Steven Butler is an actor, dancer and trained circus performer as well as a keen observer of trolls and their disgusting habits. He has starred in *The Wizard of Oz*, *Joseph and the Amazing Technicolor Dreamcoat* and as Henry in *Horrid Henry Live and Horrid!* His primary school headmaster was the fantastically funny author Jeremy Strong.

Books by Steven Butler

THE WRONG PONG
shortlisted for the Roald Dahl Funny Prize

THE WRONG PONG:
HOLIDAY HULLABALOO

THE WRONG PONG: TROLL'S TREASURE

THE WRONG PONG:
SINGIN' IN THE DRAIN

STEVEN BUTLER

Illustrated by Chris Fisher

PUFFIN

PUFFIN BOOKS

Published by the Penguin Group
Penguin Books Ltd, 80 Strand, London WC2R 0RL, England
Penguin Group (USA) Inc., 375 Hudson Street, New York, New York 10014, USA
Penguin Group (Canada), 90 Eglinton Avenue East, Suite 700, Toronto, Ontario, Canada M4P 2Y3
(a division of Pearson Penguin Canada Inc.)
Penguin Ireland, 25 St Stephen's Green, Dublin 2, Ireland (a division of Penguin Books Ltd)
Penguin Group (Australia), 250 Camberwell Road, Camberwell, Victoria 3124, Australia
(a division of Pearson Australia Group Pty Ltd)
Penguin Books India Pvt Ltd, 11 Community Centre, Panchsheel Park, New Delhi – 110 017, India
Penguin Group (NZ), 67 Apollo Drive, Rosedale, Auckland 0632, New Zealand
(a division of Pearson New Zealand Ltd)
Penguin Books (South Africa) (Pty) Ltd, Block D, Rosebank Office Park, 181 Jan Smuts Avenue,
Parktown North, Gauteng 2193, South Africa

Penguin Books Ltd, Registered Offices: 80 Strand, London WC2R 0RL, England

puffinbooks.com

First published 2012

004

Set in Baskerville MT Standard 13/19pt
Printed and bound in Great Britain by Clays Ltd, Elcograf S.p.A.

British Library Cataloguing in Publication Data
A CIP catalogue record for this book is available from the British Library

ISBN: 978–0–141–34044–9

www.greenpenguin.co.uk

For my fellow Ozians – the 2012 cast of
The Wizard of Oz at the London Palladium . . .

Edward Baker-Duly, Emma Barr, Matthew Barrow,
Marianne Benedict, Adam Bracegirdle, Lisa Bridge,
Martin Callaghan, Philip Catchpole, Tom Clark,
Kate Coysten, Owain Rhys Davies, Mike Denman,
Andrew Edwards, Sophie Evans, Russell Grant,
Tom Hargreaves, Lizzii Hills, Victoria Hinde,
Emma Housley, Luke Johnson, Tom Kanavan,
Paul Keating, Gemma Maclean, Ashley Nottingham,
Terel Nugent, Des O'Connor, Richard Roe,
Stephen Scott, Rachel Spurrell, Laura Tebbutt,
Emily Tierney, Katie Warsop, Jay Webb,
Anthony Whiteman, Anna Woodside

'Ha, Ha, Ha! Ho, Ho, Ho!'

Contents

Rubella Interrupts

Neville twitched in his sleep. He was dreaming about being Super Neville, sidekick to his favourite television hero, Captain Brilliant.

'*NEEEOOOOORRR!*' he shouted, dreaming out loud. Super Neville was soaring through the clouds, wearing his green pants of power, defeating bad guys on all sides as easily as squishing ants. He snorted, then smiled. It was great being Super Nevi–

SLAAAAAAAAAAAAAAAAAAAAAAAAAAAAAAPPP!!!

A grey-green hand swished through the air and swatted Neville straight across the face. He woke up, gasping and flailing his arms and legs like an upturned tortoise.

'*Ugh! Who's there?*'

'GET UP!' a voice grunted in the darkness as a sausage-finger poked Neville in the ribs. 'Oy!'

Neville reached over to the bedside table and fumbled for his glasses. He put them on, still not sure whether he was awake or dreaming, then flicked on the lamp.

'*AAAAAAAGH!!*' Neville nearly jumped out of his pyjamas as the sight of his enormous troll-sister, Rubella, flashed into view. Her face was so close their noses were almost touching. 'Oh! Rubella, what are you doing here?'

'Shut up, scab!' Rubella said and leered a wonky, wart-covered grimace . . . then smiled. 'D'you know I've been waiting to say that for yonkers.'

An Emergency

'What's going on?' Neville said, rubbing his pink, smarting cheek. If his mum and dad found out there was a troll in their home again, they'd scream the roof off. The last time Rubella and the Bulch family came up the toilet, they nearly destroyed his entire house. 'Why are you here, Rubella?'

'Get your thingies,' the great chunker said, frowning. 'You've got to come with me.'

Neville hesitated. He looked around his bedroom, wondering if his troll-parents, Clod and Malaria, were there too.

'WELL? COME ON!'

'Keep your voice down. Mum and Dad will go nuts.'

'Just come on!' Rubella growled, pushing her potato nose closer still.

'Why?' said Neville. He still felt like his head

was inside a pillow. 'What's wrong?'

'Get up!' Rubella snarled. She grabbed Neville's hand and yanked it.

'No!' Neville shot back. He folded his arms and tried to look as stern as he could. 'Not until you tell me what's happening.'

Rubella plonked her walrus-sized bottom on the end of Neville's bed. There was a loud creaking sound and the entire thing flipped up, catapulting Neville and his pillows across the room. He landed on a pile of stuffed toys with an *oomf*!

'It's an emergency,' Rubella said as the top end of the bed crashed back to the floor. She was still talking to the spot Neville had been lying on, not noticing that he'd shot off.

'Something terrible.'

'Oh no!' gasped Neville, clambering back to his feet. 'Is everything OK?'

Rubella spun round, puzzled to see Neville on the other side of the room. She shook her head dramatically and looked like she was about to burst into tears.

Neville's heart jumped up into his throat. Considering that in the not-too-distant past he'd seen his troll-family swallowed by a sea monster, almost got his head chewed off by a slurch with teeth like screwdrivers, discovered his grandma Joan was really an evil troll-pirate, and had to break his troll-brother, Pong, out of London Zoo . . . this must be BAD!

'There's no time to explain,' Rubella said, looking as if she was about to explode. 'I need your help, Nev.'

'OK,' said Neville, grabbing his backpack and stuffing a few changes of socks and pants into it. 'I'll be quick.' He thought about leaving a note for his parents, Marjorie and Herbert, but decided they probably wouldn't notice he was gone anyway. 'Let's go.'

Rubella grabbed Neville by the wrist and led him out of his bedroom like an angry mother and her naughty child.

'Walk faster,' Rubella urged, knocking the laundry basket over as they stormed down the hall.

Neville cringed and prayed that his sister's noisy lumbering wouldn't wake his mum and dad as she clomped towards the bathroom. Predictably, the bathroom door had been snapped across the middle and was hanging off its hinges.

'You could have been more careful.'

'I was in a hurry,' Rubella grunted. 'Now, come on. We need to get Underneath.'

Inside the bathroom, Rubella swung Neville on to her wide, sweaty back and put one foot into the toilet bowl.

'Hold on tight,' she ordered. Neville clung to the turnips sprouting from his big sister's shoulders and squeezed his eyes shut.

'Ready?'

'Ready!' said Neville.

As the toilet flushed, they were instantly sucked into soggy, pitch-blackness.

Here we go again, thought Neville as he shot round the U-bend. He never could get used to it. *Back down the loo.*

WHOOOOOOOOOOOOOOOOOOOOOOOOOSH . . .

What's Goin' On?

No matter how many times Neville went down the toilet to visit his troll-family, butterflies always gurgled in his belly whenever he arrived.

In no time at all, Rubella and Neville had flopped out of the pipes and were heading through the familiar tunnel filled with milk-bottle lanterns towards the town of Underneath. Neville gripped Rubella's shoulders and tried to ignore the nervous feeling swishing about inside him.

'Is anybody hurt?' he said into Rubella's ear. She ignored him and carried on galumphing downhill. 'Rubella?'

'*WHAT?*' Rubella snapped. 'Just shut your rat hole until we get there, OK? Can't you see I'm worryin' my noggin off, you dungle droppin'?'

Neville's jaw fell open. What on earth could have happened? He started to feel sick with concern.

What if his evil grandma, Lady Jaundice, had returned with her swashbungling crew? What if there had been a fire or a flood and the Bulch family home had been destroyed? What if someone was . . . DEAD?

Please not that!

Neville clenched his bottom, curled up his toes, scrunched his eyes tight and prayed to Captain Brilliant that no one was . . . was . . . He couldn't even think it . . .

Neither of them spoke for the rest of the journey. Neville stared, wide-eyed, as they passed beneath the stone archway with the words WELCOME UNDER carved across the top, and barely noticed the junk town beyond it.

He was way too nervous to enjoy the trip across the market square and the shortcut behind the priddle-players' bandstand. He failed to take in the trolls going this way and that or the Bulches' next-door neighbour, Gristle Pilchard, waving her walking stick and shouting 'Hello!' Neville hadn't even realized they were walking up Washing Machine Hill until Rubella plonked him down on the ground.

'Here we are,' Rubella grunted. 'This way.'

Neville shook his head and looked about, as though he was waking up all over again. They were in front of the Bulches' jam-jar house. From the top of Washing Machine Hill, Neville could see the whole town spread out below him. The sight of all the ramshackle buildings made of junk and the thousands of milk-bottle lanterns twinkling in the darkness was a beautiful one, but it didn't fill him with excitement. Although it was a relief to see it was all still there, he couldn't help worrying about what Rubella had said.

Neville turned to Rubella and was just about to question her some more when Rabies, the Bulches' giant pet troll-mole, came bounding round the edge of the house. He jumped up, resting his front paws on Neville's shoulders and slobbered all over his cheek.

'Good boy, Rabies,'

Neville said, gently nudging the enormous creature back to the ground. 'Play nicely.'

'Hurry up!' Rubella said impatiently. Then a look of concern spread across her face. 'But brace yourself, Nev . . .'

Rabies scampered away and Neville watched as his troll-sister clomped towards the green-curtained doorway. She brushed the tatty old thing aside and headed indoors.

Through the jam-jar walls, Neville could make out the blurred shapes of his troll-family. He counted them nervously.

'There's Pong,' he thought out loud as a small mottled shape skittered about on the other side of the glass. 'And that's Mooma . . .'

Neville gasped; he could see his mooma's shape bending over the big rusty stove, and Rubella flopping her backside on to a barrel seat. Pong was spinning and cartwheeling about under his mooma's feet, but where was –?

'DOODA?' Neville cried and ran through the green curtain. Something must have happened to Clod! 'DOODA! WHAT'S HAPPENED TO DOODA?'

Malaria, who was midway through stirring an enormous pan of left-sock stew, spun round and screamed. The clay pipe that hung from the corner of her mouth flew out and clattered on the floor, sending wisps of purple smoke around her feet.

'*BLLLOOOOOAAAAAAHHH!*' Pong shrieked with glee. He waddled over to where Neville stood and hugged him excitedly.

'OH MY GRACICLES!' Malaria shouted, clutching her spade-sized hands to her cheeks. 'Nev, what're you doin' 'ere, lump?' She darted towards Neville and scooped him up in a troll-hug. 'I was never expectoratin' you . . . What a squibbly surprise.'

'Where's Dooda?' Neville hugged Malaria round her thick neck. 'What's happened to him, Mooma?'

'Eh?' Malaria said.

'Just be honest,' Neville sobbed. Tears were already streaking down his cheeks. 'He's dead, isn't he?'

'What's jumbled you, Nev? You're shakin',' Malaria said, raising him to the level of her copper-coloured eyes. 'Clod's not deadsy.'

'He's not?' Neville wiped his eyes on the back of his pyjama sleeve. 'So . . . is he alive, but really, really hurt? *Arghh! What happened?*'

'Nev, pick up your pieces,' said Malaria with a surprised look on her face. She hugged him tightly. 'I don't know what whoppsy great fibbers you've been listenin' to! Dooda's fine and chuffly . . . He's snizzlin' upstairs, 'avin a nap.'

'What?' Neville said, heaving an enormous sigh of relief. He wasn't sure whether he wanted to laugh or faint. 'But, if nothing's happened to Dooda, what's the emergency?'

'Emergency?' Malaria chuckled. 'There ain't no emergency . . .'

THUD . . . THUD . . . THUD . . . THUD . . . THUD . . .

Clod appeared at the bottom of the stairs, rubbing his eyes and yawning. ''Ere, what's all this hollerin'?' he said.

'Clod, my honker,' Malaria said, beaming. 'Look who's come to visit!'

She held Neville up at arm's length.

Clod rubbed the last of the sleep from his eyes and stared for a moment. Then he focused on Neville and his face lit up into a huge, wide grin.

'NEV!' Clod yelled, jumping into the air. 'What a sight for sleepy peepers!' He thudded across the kitchen and threw his arms round Neville and Malaria. 'I'm as honkhumptious as a hump-honker.'

Neville burst into tears again. 'I'm so glad to see you!' he blubbed, planting a kiss on his dooda's rough cheek. 'I thought you were . . . I thought you were . . .'

'Go on . . . tell 'im,' said Malaria, chuckling.

'Dead,' Neville whispered.

'You thought I'd popped me conkers?' Clod laughed. 'What gave you an idea like that?'

'Well . . . it's just that Rubella told me . . .' Neville glanced at his troll-sister. She was twiddling her great stumpish thumbs at the dinner table and staring suspiciously at the floor.

'Belly told you what?' Malaria asked. She turned and looked at her daughter. 'What's goin' on?'

'Rubella woke me up and said there was an emergency,' insisted Neville.

'*WOKE YOU UP?*' Clod looked so shocked, Neville thought he might fall down. 'D'YOU MEAN TO SAY YOU'VE BEEN UP AND OUT THE TOILET? What's all this about, Rubella?'

'Nothin',' Rubella mumbled, still staring at the floor.

'What d'you mean, nothin'?' Malaria barked. 'You can't go wifflin' up the pipes on your own. Look at all the trouble Pong caused when he did it.'

Pong giggled, then copied his mooma and waggled a finger at his big sister.

'Come on, youngling,' Clod said, marching over to Rubella's side. 'Out with it!'

'I needed Nev's help.'

'What for?' said Clod.

Rubella shrugged and said nothing.

'WHAT FOR?' Malaria bellowed.

'IT'S NONE OF YOUR BUSINESS!'

'If you don't explain right now, you rambunkin' little madam,' said Clod, folding his arms, 'you'll have no seconds, or thirds, or fourths at dinner.'

Rubella sat up and stared at the rest of her family. She wasn't about to miss out on food. Her bottom lip started trembling and her face screwed up into a grimace. Then she took a deep breath, gripped hold of the edge of the dinner table, opened her mouth to speak and . . .

Rubella's Dilemma

Rubella's mouth moved so fast, Neville could barely keep up. The words poured out like water from one of the old sewer pipes.

'*IT'S-THE-AUDITIONS-FOR-THE-TOWN-PAN-TROLL-MIME-TOMORROW-AND-I-NEED-NEV-TO-HELP-ME-GET-GOOD-SO-I-CAN-BE-BETTER-THAN-GRUNTILDA!*' she screeched, barely stopping to breathe. '*WHAT-ELSE-WAS-I-SUPPOSED-TO-DO?*'

Pong burst out laughing. Everyone else just stared at the red-faced, panting troll-girl. No one spoke.

'WELL?' Rubella sobbed. She kicked at a pile of food scrapings on the floor. A mealy old teabag flew across the room and bounced off the side of Neville's head with a dull slap. '*WELL?*'

'I can't understand you,' said Neville.

'*Ugh!*' Rubella grunted. She reached into her

dress pocket and pulled out a large piece of folded paper.

'Wassat?' said Malaria.

Rubella threw the paper on to the table and Clod unfolded it. It was a brightly coloured poster, painted on the back of an old newspaper.

'Read it, Nev,' said Malaria.

Neville clambered down from his mooma's arms and walked to the table. He squinted through his glasses for a second, then read aloud . . .

'Right,' Malaria said. 'I think you need to take a big bungly breath and explain so we can all understand, Belly. I'll put on a pot of shrimp-scale tea and we'll 'ave a nice long chattywag.'

Clod pulled out a barrel seat for Neville, lifted him on to it and then sat himself down on the opposite side of the kitchen table.

'Wha's all this then?' Clod said, putting a hand on Rubella's. 'Tell ole Dooda what's up.'

'It's the auditions for the town pan-troll-mime tomorrow, and I need Nev to help me get good so I can be better than Gruntilda,' Rubella mumbled pathetically. 'She always gets the best parts.'

'Pan-troll-mime? Is it that time of yearly already?' said Clod.

'Oh, Belly,' Malaria said, lifting a rusted kettle on to the stove. 'You're a right nogginknocker sometimes!'

'Pan-troll-mime?' said Neville. Rage exploded inside him like a lit stick of dynamite and, for a split second, he forgot how afraid of Rubella he was. 'You woke me up in the middle of the night, dragged me down here and worried me half to death because you want to audition for a stupid panto?'

'IT'S NOT STUPID!' Rubella growled.

'You said it was an *emergency*.' Neville flinched away from the growling hippopotamus. 'AND WHY DID YOU ASK ME? I CAN'T HELP!'

'Well, I couldn't ask anyone else, you rottler,' said Rubella, 'otherwise Gruntilda would find out I'm going to audition.'

'But how am I supposed to help you? I don't know anything about auditioning or acting or stuff.'

'You know all about that acty-dancy-jiggedy stuff, you grubberlumper,' Rubella said, pointing an accusing sausage-finger at Neville. 'I saw the picture on the shelf last time we all came to stay at your house.'

Neville opened his mouth to protest, but stopped himself. He knew exactly which picture Rubella was talking about. It was a photograph above the mantelpiece of him and his classmates in the school play.

'It was only the school nativity,' Neville said. 'I don't know –'

'Exactly!' interrupted Rubella, clapping her hands together. 'You know all about it . . . *aaand* . . . no one else talks to YOU, so I'll surprise them all.'

'But I only played a sheep!' Neville insisted. 'And I wasn't even a very good sheep.' His tummy gurgled at the memory of wearing his scratchy costume and trying to remember all the words to 'Away in a Manger', and all those mums and dads staring. 'I'm not a performer, Rubella.'

'SHUT UP!' Rubella shouted. 'You know more than anyone else I could ask and you're goin' to tell me everythin' you know, or . . . or . . . I'LL YANK YOUR EARS OFF!'

'Ha ha!' Clod beamed. 'Our Belly wantin' to be a star! How exciterous. What show is it?'

'*Whingerella*,' said Rubella.

'OH, I LOVE THAT ONE!' shouted Clod.

'*Whingerella*? Like *Cinderella*?' Neville was getting more and more angry. 'But you said it was an *emergency*.'

'It is,' Rubella cried, smacking her hand dramatically across her forehead. 'Gruntilda . . . You remember her?'

Neville racked his brains . . . She was Rubella's bony friend that he'd met the very first time he'd journeyed down the toilet to the Underneath.

He nodded.

'Gruntilda's mum is in charge of the pan-troll-mime,' Rubella said, leaning in like she was sharing a deep dark secret. 'If I'm not extra good, Gruntilda will get the best part in the show . . . BUT I WANT TO PLAY IT!'

'You want to play Whingerella?' Neville asked.

'UGH! NO!' Rubella barked. 'No one likes Whingerella. I want to be the grumptious stepsister that wears the grass slipper and marries the prince.'

'I thought there were two stepsisters,' said Neville. He was starting to get confused.

'Not in *Whingerella*,' said Rubella. 'Everyone knows that the grumptious stepsister is far too grumptious for there to be more than one . . . I'm grumptious and I want to get all smoochery with the prince.'

'Oh!' said Clod. His grey-green cheeks started to blush. 'I . . . erm . . .'

'Who's playin' old princey-poo?' asked Malaria, trying not to laugh. She handed out a tray full of mugs of steaming tea.

'Thicket!' Rubella said. 'He plays it every yearly.' She turned an odd shade of pink and almost swooned off her seat. 'He's the thorniest boy in the whole town.'

Neville thought he might throw up. Yuck! The thought of having to kiss Rubella was enough to make someone sick for a whole week. Poor Thicket! Neville had never seen his troll-sister like this. Normally she was smashing things or bursting through walls or getting into fights. He'd never seen her act so . . . well . . . girly!

'In that case,' Clod said, rubbing his hands together excitedly, 'we'd better make sure you're tippy-top and the best beauty-beamer up on that stage, Belly.'

'That sounds just squibbly, it does,' Malaria joined in. 'Our Belly, a princess.'

Rubella turned to Neville. 'What d'ya say, Nev?' she said, smiling through gritted teeth. Neville was still angry and wanted to say no, but he noticed his troll-sister's club-like hands balled up into fists. He nodded slowly.

'Right then,' said Clod. 'What's first?'

Everyone looked at Neville expectantly. He didn't know what to say.

'Well, um . . .' Neville tried to remember the pantomime his friend Archie's mum had taken them to. 'I suppose –'

'Don't suppose, Nev,' snapped Rubella. She mimed pulling his ears off across the table.

'DANCING!' Neville said with a gulp. 'You should practise some dancing.'

'EASY!' Rubella barked and darted up the stairs, mumbling to herself. 'I'll just get my . . .'

Neville wrinkled his brow. He hadn't quite caught the end of Rubella's sentence, but . . . a twinge of fear crept up his spine. Surely he was going mad? Neville could have sworn he just heard Rubella say, 'I'll just get my . . . TUTU!'

Meanwhile

Somewhere, in one of the big houses on the other side of town, Gruntilda Bunt stood in the middle of a large room made from rusty old train carriages.

'One, two, three and up,' the troll-girl puffed. 'One, two, three and up.' She was doing knee bends and arm twirls. 'Can I stop now?' she called in her snickery little voice. 'Moomsie? Can I stop now?'

The door burst open and the shape of a tall, thin troll-woman emerged from the next room.

'WHAT?'

'My arms are pooped,' Gruntilda whinged.

Her twiggy hair creaked as she bobbed up and down. 'Look!' She gave a little yelp as she spun her bony arms to show just how tired she was.

The troll in the doorway scowled, then smiled the kind of smile you'd see on a slurch right before it ate you. 'Dunklin', you have to make sure you're the best at the pan-troll-mime auditions or Moomsie won't love you any more . . . You don't want Moomsie not to love you, do you?'

Gruntilda shook her head.

'THEN SHUT UP AND PRACTISE!'

Practice

'A bit more round the ankle,' Rubella whined. She sat on one of the barrel seats and wriggled her foot in the air. 'Come on, Nev.'

Neville could hardly believe what he was about to do. He glanced down at the bucket of oven grease in his hands and choked back the sour taste that rose into his mouth.

'NEV, YOU WHELP! A BIT MORE GREASE ON MY ANKLE!' Rubella yelled. She was sitting there, bulging half in and half out of a pink frilly tutu. 'I CAN'T GET IN MY TIGHTS . . . AND IF I CAN'T GET THEM ON I CAN'T PRACTISE MY DANCE!'

Neville jolted, but didn't seem able to make his arms and legs work. He couldn't help but gawp at his troll-sister's grey-green rump, spilling out through the seams in all directions. It was like a bulldozer trying on a handkerchief.

'Oh, Belly, you're goin' to look grumptious.' Malaria chuckled, tugging at the tutu's straps and heaving the pink material over the turnips on Rubella's shoulders. 'A proper dainty-dinklet.'

'OY!' Rubella kicked Neville in the leg. 'GET ON WITH IT!'

Neville slowly scooped up a great globule of grease and, with shaking hands, approached the enormous leg that dangled in front of him. He reached out and touched the hairy ankle like someone poking a deadly snake, then smeared the dinner-smelling sludge up and down it before he retched.

'It's about time,' Rubella snapped, shoving Neville aside. The bucket of grease *CLANG-ANG-ANG*ed across the floor, spilling its contents in a big yellowish pool. Pong cooed wildly, took a run up and slid through it on his stomach.

'*CCCCOOOOOOOOOOOOOOOOOOOOOOHHHH!*'

'All righty,' said Clod, who'd been watching from the corner with a happy grin on his face. 'Let's get those tighties on you, Belly.' He grabbed the top of Rubella's tights and yanked them upwards.

'PULL!' Malaria shouted. 'HEAVE!' She joined in and grabbed hold of the other side. Neville watched in complete horror as his mooma and dooda huffed and groaned. The pink woollen tights were close to bursting and they were barely beyond Rubella's feet.

'Breathe in,' Clod wheezed, pulling harder and harder at the waistband.

'I AM BREATHING IN!' Rubella barked. 'MAYBE WE NEED MORE GREASE?'

'There *is* no more grease,' Neville said, keeping out of his troll-sister's kicking range.

'PULL!' Malaria ordered again. She and Clod were tugging so hard at the pink tights that Rubella had to grip hold of the barrel she was sitting on to stop herself from being hoisted into the air.

'Don't just stand there,' Rubella hissed at Neville. 'HELP!'

Neville didn't know what to do. Rubella's tutu was like a trap that was about to spring open at any moment. He could hear ripping noises coming from somewhere under her gargantuan bottom.

'Almost there!' wheezed Clod.

Suddenly there was an enormous *SNAAAAAAAAP* and the tights and tutu sprang into place. Clod and Malaria both tumbled to the floor in a heap of grey-green arms and legs.

'Ha!' Rubella blurted, then did a twirl. The tutu was such a squeeze that Rubella's gut was forced upwards and sat beneath her chin like a mildewed, warty pillow.

'OOOHH, WE DID IT!' Malaria cheered from the floor. 'PRINCESS BELLY OF WASHING MACHINE HILL!'

Neville looked at the horror in front of him and

felt the urge to run away and hide.

'You look like a right honker, Belly,' Clod said as he clambered back to his feet. 'Absolutely wonderbunkin' . . . Don't she, Nev?'

Neville almost screamed. How could his dooda think she looked wonderful? He turned to Rubella and nodded, somehow managing not to pull a face. Maybe Neville was a better actor than he thought he was.

'Righty-ho, Belly,' said Malaria. She scooped Pong up from the grease puddle on the floor and sat down with him on one of the barrels. 'Let's see then.'

Neville's heart started to race. He dived on to the seat next to his mooma. This was it . . . Rubella was about to perform.

CLLOOOOOOOOOOMMMMMMMMPPPPPP!!!

Neville barely had time to duck behind Malaria.

THHUUUUUUUUUUDDDDDDDDDDDDDD!!!

Rubella started clattering about the kitchen, a great pink mass of flapping arms and pounding feet. She twirled on the spot and stuck one leg out to the side, toppling a stack of dirty plates as she passed.

'Yeah!' whooped Clod. 'Go on, my lump.' He started whistling a tune and clapping his hands while his daughter hammered back and forth like a wrecking ball.

'WATCH, NEV!' Rubella yelled as she manoeuvred through a bunch of high leaps and groany lunges. Neville stared in total shock. Watch? He couldn't look away even if he wanted to.

Every time Rubella landed from one of her enormous jumps, her spade-sized feet left large holes in the floor.

CRRAAAAAAAAAAAAAAAAAACCCKKKKKK!!!

Rubella leapt straight up into the air and put her head through the ceiling. She dangled there in a cloud of broken plaster and splintered boards.

'How squibbly,' Malaria said, turning to smile at Neville. 'I've never seen such a heart-hobblin' performance.'

Rubella's head seemed to have got stuck. She hung there like a headless, overstuffed windsock, swinging her tree-trunk legs this way and that.

'GET READY FOR THE BIG FINISH!'

Rubella's voice shouted down from the floor above.

Neville held his breath.

Pong clapped wildly and screamed.

CCRRRRAAAAAAAAAAAASSSSSSSSSHHHHHH!!!

Rubella finally came plummeting back towards the kitchen floor and landed doing the splits with all the grace of a grand piano dropped from the top of a building.

'TA-DAH!'

Clod and Malaria jumped to their feet and applauded the sweaty boulder in front of them.

'How's about that then?' said Rubella, staggering back to her feet. 'Wha' d'you reckon, Nev?'

Neville tried to smile. It was so much worse than he'd expected.

'It's very good,' he lied. 'I don't think you need my help.'

'Nonkumbumps,' declared Malaria. 'You're a handy thing to 'ave about, Nev. What with all your yearlies of theatrics.'

Neville groaned. This was terrible . . . Rubella was *terrible*! *THE WHOLE THING WAS TERRIBLE!*

'What else?' asked Rubella.

'Well,' said Neville. 'You should probably practise your singing. Pantomimes normally have songs.'

'Oh, there ain't no nevermind there, Nev,' said Clod. 'Belly's got the voice of a birdy.'

'Yeah, a vulture,' Neville whispered to himself.

'What?' Rubella scowled.

'Nothing!' Neville said. 'I'd love to hear it.'

'Go on, Belly,' said Malaria, hugging Pong tightly. 'Sing that thingy . . . y'know . . . the thingy about the . . . thingy.'

'Oh, that one,' Rubella said casually. 'Yeah, all right.'

All across the town of Underneath, trolls going about their daily lives staggered to a sudden halt as an ear-splitting screech echoed through the

darkness, shattering every milk-bottle lantern within three blocks of the Bulches'.

'That were lovely,' said Clod, wiping a small tear from the corner of his eye.

'I know,' said Rubella. She folded her arms over her giant pink gut and twiddled her hair. 'What did you think, Nev?'

Neville wasn't listening. His ears were ringing and he seemed to be the only person that had noticed the entire side-wall of the kitchen exploding outwards down the hill. He gawped and stared with wide eyes.

'He's overwhelped,' said Malaria. She wandered over and patted Neville lovingly on the head. 'I think you've got a fan, Belly.'

In the Morning

The ticker-dinger-thinger, a giant troll-clock in the market square, *BAAAANGED* its morning bang and echoed across the town. Neville jolted awake and tumbled out on to Rubella's bedroom floor like an oversized rag doll.

'Ugh! Hello?' he said, yawning. Neville had been fast asleep in his usual spot on top of Rubella's laundry pile. He rubbed his eyes, then looked around the messy room. Rubella wasn't in her hammock.

'Belly?' Neville called. Her pink tights and tutu were in a heap on the other side of the room and the bedroom door was wide open. Neville caught the familiar scent of moss cakes and warm pickled fisheyes drifting upstairs from the kitchen. How long had he slept?

Quickly untangling his legs from a large pair of

Rubella's knickers, Neville headed across the room and down the stairs. His tummy felt strange, but he wasn't sure if hunger or nerves about the day ahead were the cause.

'Here he is!' Clod beamed as Neville reached the bottom step. 'We were startin' to think you weren't comin' down at all.'

'Mornin', my snizzler,' said Malaria. 'You're gettin' all lazy like your sister, you are. I'm so chuffly.'

'Sorry,' Neville said, yawning again. He was exhausted. Rubella had insisted they stay up for half the night practising her singing. After what seemed like hours, Neville had finally convinced her to sing a little more quietly and not shatter the remaining walls with her wailing, which at least felt like a bit of progress.

'I don't believe you, Nev!' Rubella grunted. 'You were supposed to help me get ready.'

Neville looked at his big troll-sister and stumbled off the last step in surprise. He wasn't sure how many shocks he could take in such a short space of time.

Rubella had a new outfit on. She was wearing

a dress like the flamenco dancers Neville had seen on his mum's favourite TV show. The top half of it was bright putrid green with sparkly bottle-tops sewn round the collar, and there was a frilly purple skirt, which was short at the front and flowing at the back. She looked like a nightmarish peacock.

'You look just like one of them princessy types, Belly,' Malaria said, chuckling. She twisted Rubella's bristly hair into a bun and tucked an old dead flower into it for extra princessliness.

'I KNOW!' Rubella snapped. 'OF COURSE I DO.'

Neville looked at his troll-sister and felt his heart sinking. If she didn't get the part she wanted in the pan-troll-mime, she'd blame him and yank his ears off. What was he going to do?

'How's about a wee snifflet of breakfast, Nev?' said Clod, offering up a plate of moss cakes.

Neville reached out to take one, but Rubella's great warty hand grabbed his wrist before he could.

'I don't think so,' Rubella said. She had rosy painted cheeks and bright red lips that made her look even more demented than usual. 'Eat later . . . We've got to get a move on, whelp. COME ON!'

With that, Rubella disappeared through the green curtain like a runaway circus tent, dragging Neville behind her.

La La Laaaa!!!

By the time Neville and Rubella reached the theatre in the centre of town, there was already a long line of hopeful young trolls shuffling nervously outside. Each and every one was dressed in an elaborate gown or suit made from all sorts of sewn-together rags and tatters.

'Guh!' Rubella huffed. She was out of breath from all the hurrying and sweating like a bullock on a bonfire. 'This is your fault, Nev!' She swished her

flamenco skirt at Neville, almost knocking him off his feet.

'We'll have to wait,' Neville said, as the thought of Rubella yanking his ears off crossed his mind again. 'Anyway . . . the longer we spend in line, the longer you have to warm up and be really good.'

Rubella raised her hand to swat Neville aside – then thought about what he'd just said and lowered it again.

'Fine,' she humphed, then started practising scales along with all the other eager performers. The noise was awful; not a single troll in the line could sing in tune. It was like listening to a thousand nails being scratched down a chalkboard. Maybe Rubella might have a better chance than Neville had first thought?

Slowly, step by step, the line moved along, and Neville and Rubella eventually passed through the big double doors of the town theatre. Neville hadn't been inside this building since his first-ever trip to the Underneath and he'd forgotten how big it was.

The high walls were made from row upon row of tin cans that shone dully in the gloom and, high above, a chandelier made from hundreds of twisted knives and forks gleamed impressively. Neville felt a tingle of excitement creep down the back of his neck. He loved going to the theatre . . . even if this one was a stinking troll-theatre.

'Rubella,' Neville whispered. 'It's *amazing*.'

'Shut up,' hissed Rubella. 'A princess needs to find her inner grumptiousness.'

Neville had to hold back a groan. The only way Rubella could find a grumptious inner princess was if she ate one.

Ahead of them, the line of trolls went down the side of a steep bank of wonky, muddled chairs and tatty sofas that descended towards a big stage.

'LOOK!' Rubella gasped, pointing to the troll at the front of the queue. Neville recognized him instantly. It was Thicket with a thorn briar growing

out of his back and a bolt through his left nostril. 'You better have trained me proper, Nev.'

Neville gulped and distracted himself by looking at the stage. It was enormous and lit from either side by two massive glass jars filled with giant buzzing insects. They were like huge wasps, but their stripes glowed like purple fire and cast eerie pools of light on the stage as they jostled about.

'Rubella,' Neville whispered again, 'what are those things?'

Rubella stopped in the middle of a particularly high note and grimaced at Neville.

'WHAT?'

'Those big waspy things,' said Neville. 'What are they?'

'*Scrawnets!*' she snapped. 'Everyone's seen a scrawnet before. NOW STOP RUININ' MY CONCENTRATION! If I don't get the part of the grumptious stepsister, it's your fault . . . AND YOU KNOW WHAT I'LL DO!'

Neville clamped his mouth shut and took a step away from his singing troll-sister. This was bad . . . really bad.

Meanwhile

Behind the curtain at the back of the stage, Gruntilda peeked through a rip at all the other trolls gathering to audition. There were so many of them.

'Now, Gruntilda,' a voice said behind her, 'it's time to make the Bunt family proud.'

Gruntilda turned and smiled a snake-like smile at her mooma.

'I can't wait, Moomsie,' Gruntilda sneered.

'Good . . . Then get out of my way!' replied Gruntilda's mooma, sweeping past her with a flourish and slinking through the curtain on to the stage. 'It's showtime!'

Abominatia Bunt

The whole theatre went silent as the tall, thin troll stepped on to the stage and struck a dramatic pose in the spotlight. She was like no troll Neville had ever seen before.

Where the Bulches were round and squashy, this troll-lady was long and spiky. She wore a tight black dress made from bin liners that went all the way down to the floor and rustled as she walked. Her hair was a tower of Venus fly-traps piled high on her head, and ivy grew from her shoulders, hanging down on either side of her neck like the trollish version of a feather boa.

'Who's that?' Neville asked quietly. Something about the troll-woman made him feel very nervous.

'Who d'ya think, foozle fart?' said Rubella, planting her fists on her boulder-sized hips. 'That's Gruntilda's mooma. She's blunkin' famous.'

Neville spotted Gruntilda shuffling about in the shadows behind her mooma.

'WELCOME!' the woman announced to the crowd. She gestured with her arms as if she wanted to hug the entire theatre and tossed her ivy from side to side. 'I'M ABOMINATIA BUNT AND I'M SO HAPPY TO SEE YOU ALL.'

'Yeah, right,' Rubella grumbled under her breath.

A few nervous murmurs came from the crowd, while some others waved or nodded. One overeager young troll even threw a bunch of swamp-flowers at her. Abominatia looked down at the bouquet as if she'd just discovered an unexpected foozle dropping in her path. 'How lummy.' She grimaced and kicked them aside. 'Shall we get started?'

She clapped her hands, and four important-looking trolls stepped out on to the stage. Neville recognized one of them. It was Glottel Potch the town mayor.

'Those are the judges,' whispered Rubella.

A short, pot-bellied troll, wearing a sewn-together catsuit, sweatband and legwarmers, dashed on to the stage from the wings.

'RIGHTY-HO, UNDERLINGS,' he shouted to the crowd, flailing his arms dramatically. He was holding a clipboard. 'MY NAME IS MUCUS, CHOREOGRAPHER AND ASSISTANT TO MRS –'

'MISS!' Abominatia screeched. She looked like someone had just punched her in the stomach.

'Sorry,' said Mucus. 'MISS! ASSISTANT TO

MISS BUNT. WHEN I CALL YOUR NAMIES, YOU HAVE TO COME UP THROUGH THE CURTAIN HERE AND SHOW US WHAT TALENT-TOOTERS YOU ALL ARE . . . OK?'

The crowd remained silent and just stared at the chubby little troll.

'OK, then . . .' he said with a fixed smile on his face. 'First up, we have . . .'

NEXT!

'NEEEEEEXXTT!'

One after another, trolls were called up onstage to show off their talent to Abominatia. She was luxuriously draped on a sofa at the front like a Hollywood star from one of Neville's mum's magazines. Next to her were Gruntilda, Thicket and the panel of important-looking trolls.

Neville took a seat at the back and watched with a mixture of fear and delight as everyone waited for their turn.

'NEXT!' Abominatia screamed at a jittery troll-girl when she was halfway through her love song, 'My Toadstools Grow For You!' The girl burst into floods of tears and ran offstage.

Neville heaved a sigh of relief. Most of the other trolls auditioning had been absolutely terrible. He'd already watched priddle players twangling noisily, a slurch charmer, an old troll named Bowel reciting troll-poetry, a troll-girl trying to balance a fridge on the end of her nose and a teenage troll-boy, who juggled the rest of his family. It had all seemed to be going quite well until he'd accidentally thrown his grandmooma through the side-wall of the theatre.

A young troll with ears of corn sprouting from his shoulders ambled onstage next.

'Hello and what's your name?' Abominatia asked wearily.

'Erm . . . Stump,' said Stump.

'And what are you going to do for us, Stump?' Abominatia half said, half yawned. She looked utterly bored and pulled a left sock from her pocket and started chewing on it.

'Well . . . um . . . I do tricks with Dumbly.'

'Who's Dumbly?'

'Dumbly's my pet –'

Before Stump could finish, an enormous dungle lumbered on to the stage. It clattered to the centre, where it scraped its hooves and tossed its horned head from side to side viciously.

Mucus threw his clipboard into the air,

screamed and dived over the back of his sofa.

Gruntilda laughed hysterically.

'This is Dumbly,' Stump announced to the entire theatre. Then he turned to the immense beast and held up his hand. 'SIT, DUMBLY, SIT!'

Dumbly didn't sit. It just snorted great nostrilfuls of steam at the young troll.

'ROLL OVER!' Stump said. 'ROLL OVER, DUMBLY!'

Dumbly didn't roll over either. Instead, it lowered its horns and started growling. Neville crossed his fingers and squinted. This was the first time he'd ever seen a real-live dungle and it didn't look like it was going to end well.

'JUMP, DUMBLY!' Stump yelled. 'OY, YOU BUNGLER! JU–'

Dumbly suddenly charged across the stage and butted Stump high into the air. As the crowds of auditioning trolls started cheering, the young troll landed with an *oomf* back to front on the dungle's shoulders.

'ABOMINATIA!' Stump called as his pet galloped off through the hole left by the juggled grandmooma. 'I'M YOUR WHOPPSIEST FAN!'

'NEXT!' screamed Abominatia.

There was a long pause, one of the curtains twitched and then a mountain in a green-and-purple flamenco dress clomped onstage. Neville caught his breath. It was Rubella . . .

The Audition

'Hello,' said Abominatia, glaring at Rubella as if it caused her pain.

''Ello,' said Rubella, fiddling nervously with the frills on her sleeve. Neville watched his troll-sister through his fingers, praying to Captain Brilliant that she would perform well.

'And what are you going to do?'

'Well . . . um . . .' said Rubella. 'I'm goin' to do a bit of everythin'.'

'Everything?'

'Yep.' Rubella nodded. 'I'm a singing-ballerina-princess type.' She batted her crusty eyelashes at Thicket in the front row.

'Rubella Bulch, a ballerina?' Gruntilda giggled. '*More like a barrel-ina!*'

Rubella scrunched up her face and scowled. 'Just you watch, Gruntilda.' Then she leapt into action.

The entire theatre went silent as everyone watched Rubella jiggle this way and that. She swung her hips in circles and shimmied her colossal belly up and down, all the while hammering out high notes like an over-boiled kettle.

Neville didn't know what to think. He couldn't tell if Rubella's performance was absolutely awful or absolutely brilliant.

'MY PEEPERS!' cried the old troll Bowel as one of the bottle-tops on Rubella's dress flew off and pinged him in the face.

'*OOOOOOOOH-EEEEEEEEH-OOOOOOOOH!!!*'

Rubella whipped off the purple skirt to reveal some sparkly pants made from tinfoil and sticky tape, as she went into a series of high kicks.

'YEAH!' cried Neville, trying to drum up support for his troll-sister. 'GO ON, RUBELLA!'

Rubella didn't need to be asked twice. In no time

she was tapping out rhythms with her uncut toenails, while flapping her arms up and down.

Neville couldn't believe it . . . the crowd started cheering for her.

'*WAAAAAAAA-WEEEEEEEE-WAAAAAAAA!!!*'

As her grand finale, Rubella dived through the air as if trying to catch an invisible ball – and smashed straight through the centre of the stage.

Everyone waited. The entire theatre held its breath and stared at the great hole in the floor and the cloud of dust rising from it. Then, after a long pause, Rubella poked her head up through the hole and smiled a big I'm-proud-of-myself smile.

Everyone, including Thicket and Mucus, burst into wild applause.

'SHE'S AMAZEROUS!'

'THAT WAS INCREDIBUMP!'

'*AAAAAARGGGHHHH!!!!*'

Abominatia and Gruntilda looked appalled.

'That's quite enough of that,' Abominatia barked. 'SILENCE!'

The auditorium went quiet. Everyone, including Rubella, who was clambering out of the hole in the stage, gazed at the rake-thin director. She looked furious and one of her flytraps had wilted and was dangling in front of her face, snapping wildly. She brushed it away, smoothed her bin-liner dress and smiled.

'Thank you, Rubungle,' Abominatia said to Rubella. 'That'll be all.'

'It's Rubella,' said Rubella, but Abominatia wasn't listening. Rubella stomped offstage, dragging her purple skirt behind her. 'GUH!'

'And now the moment I'm sure you've all been waiting for,' Abominatia announced to the whole theatre. She started to fan herself as if she couldn't cope with the excitement. 'My grumptious grumplet is going to do her audition. The most talent-tooting troll in the whole of the Underneath . . . GRUNTILDA BUNT!'

Gruntilda jumped to her feet and flung her arms into the air as if expecting a wave of applause. 'Thank you,' she shouted. 'THANK YOU!'

No one clapped.

Gruntilda humphed loudly, pulled a face at the audience and skulked up on to the stage.

''Ere we go,' a voice suddenly whispered in Neville's ear. Neville spun round to see Rubella sitting in the row behind him, having just sneaked back through the theatre. 'Little Missy Princess Plop.'

'You were great, Rubella,' Neville whispered. 'I think.'

'I know,' Rubella said with a grin. 'This yearly, I have to beat that bag-o-bones.'

Neville winked at his troll-sister, then turned back to look at Gruntilda on the stage. The skinny troll took a deep breath, struck a pose and started to sing.

'OW!' Neville yelped, covering his ears. The noise was a whiny, high-pitched squeal, like someone blowing on a broken whistle.

'*BLAAAAAAAAAAAAAAAAAAAAAAAAAAGH!*'

All the trolls in the audience began to groan and hold their hands over their ears.

'LA-LA-LA-LAAAAAAA-LA-LA-LAAA!'

Gruntilda's face turned bright red. She looked like a cocktail stick with a tomato jammed on the end.

'FUH-FUH-FUH-FUH-FUH-FUH-FUH!'

Neville couldn't believe it. He thought Rubella was a bad singer, but Gruntilda was DREADFUL. He watched as one of the important-looking judges toppled backwards off his seat.

'*OOOOOOOOOOOOOOOOOOOOHHH!*'

She finished her song with a howling, painful top note that echoed off the tin-can walls and made them shake. Neville thought his ears were going to drop off, it was so horrible to listen to.

Then there was silence . . .

Everyone looked at Gruntilda in total shock. She did a wobbly curtsey, giggled and skipped offstage with a look of utter triumph on her ratty little face.

'WONDERBUNK!' Abominatia shouted, standing up and clapping wildly. 'SUCH TALENT!' She walked back on to the stage and turned to face everyone. 'THANK YOU, ONE AND ALL. NOW THE JUDGES WILL GO AND CAST THEIR VOTES TO DECIDE WHO PLAYS WHAT IN THIS YEARLY'S PAN-TROLL-MIME. THE RESULTS WON'T BE LONG . . . IT'S GOING TO BE HUMDIFFEROUS!'

Neville had never felt so relieved. Gruntilda was so bad that Rubella was sure to get the best part. Maybe he wouldn't get his ears yanked off after all.

Meanwhile

In a small storeroom at the side of the theatre, Abominatia Bunt stamped back and forth, rustling as she went. She was fuming with rage.

Snatching up a scorecard from the table, she looked at it again and howled. She was so angry her bony hand was shaking. How? How did that rhinoceros Bulch girl beat her wonderbunkin' daughter?

Then something suddenly occurred to her, and she stopped stamping. *I'm the only underling that's seen the final result.*

Making sure that no one was

looking, Abominatia ripped the card in half and stuffed the pieces deep into a box of tatty old costumes.

'Bye-bye, Bulchy,' she whispered sneeringly to herself. Then she checked that her flytrap hair tower was beautifully in place, smoothed her bin liners and slunk off, muttering, 'No one outperforms a Bunt. NO ONE!'

Results

The waiting was unbearable. Neville stood in the corner of the stage while Rubella scuffed backwards and forwards, murmuring to herself. Everyone was keen to find out who was in the pan-troll-mime and which unlucky fuzzbonks didn't make the cut.

'Come on,' Rubella grumbled. 'Hurry up.'

Neville looked at his troll-sister and sighed. He couldn't help but feel sorry for the great big lardy-lumper. She was desperate to be the grumptious stepsister.

'It's all right,' Neville said, as Rubella trudged past. 'I'm sure it won't be much longer.' At least he hoped it wouldn't. The longer Rubella had to wait, the grumpier she got, and if it turned out to be bad news . . . Neville gulped. He didn't want to think about it.

Suddenly, the troll-girl who'd balanced a fridge on the end of her nose jumped up and pointed. 'LOOK!'

Everyone turned to see what was happening.

Abominatia swished her way round the back curtain and smiled at everyone with the kind of smile you'd give someone who didn't realize they had food dribbling down their chin. It was a mixture of pity and disgust.

'Ladies and gentlegeorges,' she said, brandishing a scrap of paper. 'Here are the results of the pan-troll-mime auditions.'

Neville watched as the troll-skeleton walked over to the side of the stage and pinned the paper to the wall with a rusty nail.

'Goodly luck,' she sneered, and swished off back behind the curtains.

'Quick!' Rubella snapped at Neville as everyone jumped up and crowded towards the notice. Neville darted ahead and reached it before anybody else.

'What's it say, Nev?' Rubella shouted above the din of trolls scrabbling over each other.

Everyone went silent as Neville pulled the paper off the wall and cleared his throat.

‘Ahem . . . um . . .’ Neville really wasn’t sure he wanted to do this, but he looked down at the paper nonetheless and read aloud:

‘Whingerella – Who cares?
The Narra-troll – Bowel Bumble
The Furry Bog-mother – Gristle Pilchard
The Prince – Thicket Ulcer-tooth’

‘Totally grotsome,’ shouted Thicket, punching the air and jumping. ‘I knew it!’

‘How chuffly,’ cried Gristle Pilchard. Neville couldn’t see her, but he could just about make out her walking stick waving in the air near the back of the group. ‘Congruntulations, Bowel!’

‘Squibbly,’ Bowel shouted back. He hobbled out of the group and did a little bow. ‘I’ve never been a narra-troll before!’

‘Who else?’ shouted Rubella. ‘Who’s the grumptious stepsister?’

Neville glanced down the list, found where it said ‘Grumptious Stepsister’ and froze. Oh no! Gruntilda’s name had been written next to the part. Rubella was going to be so angry.

'WHO IS IT, NEV?'

Neville could feel beads of sweat breaking out on his forehead. Things couldn't get any wor–

Before he'd even had time to think *Things couldn't get any worse*, they did. His entire body started to tremble as he spotted Rubella's name at the bottom of the list – and saw the role she'd been given in the pan-troll-mime.

Without a second's thought, Neville dropped the paper on the ground and RAN!

Bad News

'Nev, my lump!' Clod beamed as Neville raced into the kitchen through the green curtain. 'How'd it go?'

'HIDE ME!' Neville yelped, darting behind Clod's back and scrunching himself up as small as he could.

'Hide you?' Clod chuckled. 'What're you hidin' from?'

'What do you think?' Neville said, pointing through the jam-jar walls to the enormous shape of Rubella lumbering up Washing Machine Hill. Neville hid his face in his hands and hummed the Captain Brilliant theme tune to himself. This was it – the moment his brute of a big troll-sister would finish him off.

Malaria came downstairs with Pong riding on her shoulders.

'Oh, Nev,' she said, putting the little troll down at the dinner table. 'Is Belly done already? I'm so exciterous to hear how it went!'

'Erm,' said Clod. 'I'm not sure there's such squibbly news.' He scooped Neville up and squeezed him in a troll-hug.

'She's going to kill me,' Neville whimpered.

'Oh, nonkumbumps,' said Malaria. 'Why would Belly go and do a thing like that? What's occurinatin'?'

'I think we're about to find out,' Clod said, nodding to the curtained front door.

Rubella burst through, sweaty-faced and scowling.

'WHERE IS HE?' she bellowed, looking crazily around the kitchen. 'I'M GOIN' TO SQUISH HIM!'

'IT'S NOT MY FAULT!' Neville yelled, then instantly buried his face in the fold of Clod's arm.

'YES, IT IS!' Rubella shouted back. She ripped the flower out of her hair and threw it on the floor. 'YOU MUST HAVE TRAINED ME WRONG!'

'Belly,' snapped Malaria. 'You ain't squishin' Nev, so you can be forgettin' about it right now.'

'What's wrong?' Clod asked. 'Didn't you get into the pan-troll-mime?'

Rubella's mouth curled down at the edges and her bottom lip started to tremble.

'Oh, my honker,' Malaria said and put an arm round Rubella's shoulders. 'It's nothin' to go worry-wartin' about.'

'Yep,' said Clod. 'Just cos you ain't in the pan-troll-mime, it don't make you any less of a jumbly-Jennifer to us.'

'It's not that,' Neville said in a tiny voice.

'Not what?' asked Clod.

'It's not that Rubella didn't get a part.'

'Well, what's goin' on then?' Malaria said. 'Are you in? Are you the grumptious stepsister?'

'NO!' Rubella burst out crying.

'Oh no . . .' said Clod, screwing up his face and sticking his tongue out. 'Are you Whingerella? That's a pooky part.'

'NO!' Rubella wailed. 'IT'S WORSE THAN THAT!'

'What are you then?' said Malaria.

'I'M . . .'

'Yes?'

'I'M . . .'

'Oh, spit it out, Belly,' said Malaria, rolling her eyes. 'I've got to put din-dins on in a winky bit.'

'I'M THE TURNIP THAT GETS TURNED

INTO A COACH!' Rubella screamed.

'Oh.' Malaria coughed back a laugh. 'I like turnips.'

'IT'S DREADSY!'

'No, it ain't,' said Clod. 'I'm sure you'll make a lummy turnip.'

'WHAT?' Rubella looked like she was going to rocket off through the ceiling.

'Dooda's right,' Neville added, trying his hardest to smile. 'I'm sorry you didn't get the part you wanted, Rubella, but I bet you'll be brilliant . . . and if it makes you feel better, I thought you were terrific today.'

'NO, IT DOESN'T MAKE ME FEEL BETTER!' Rubella stamped her feet and turned away.

'Who's playing the grumptious stepsister?' Malaria asked Neville.

'Gruntilda Bunt,' said Neville. 'She was awful; I don't know how the judges picked her.'

'That bony, snickerty, twiglin' of a skinnifer!' Rubella yelled. 'I hope her branches break.'

'Now, Belly,' said Clod, in his Dooda-knows-best voice, 'I'm sure she got the part fairy squarey.'

Rubella glared at Clod, then at Neville, and grunted.

'Well,' Neville said after a long moment of awkward silence. 'I suppose I should be getting back up the toilet now it's all over. Mum and Dad will be wondering where I've got to.'

Neville climbed down from Clod's arms and hugged his dooda's knee. 'Bye, Dooda.'

'Bye, Nev,' said Clod, planting a kiss on Neville's head. 'Come again soon, won't you.'

Neville nodded and smiled. He turned to go and hug his mooma, when one of Rubella's enormous feet stuck out and blocked his path.

'Oh, no you don't,' Rubella hissed, bending down and shoving her nose against Neville's like Dumbly the angry dungle. 'If I'm stuck bein' a stonkin' great turnip, you're stuck here with me.'

'What?' Neville gasped. Butterflies suddenly rose up in his stomach.

'I ain't doin' this on my own,' said Rubella. 'There's loads of other parts in the pan-troll-mime. If I've got to do it, you're doin' it too.'

'But, I . . .' Neville stammered. 'I want to go home.'

'TOUGH TONSILS!' growled Rubella and flicked him on the end of his nose with her stumpy finger.

Clod clapped his hands together.

'Two younglings in the pan-troll-mime,' he said with a chuckle. 'How squibbly.'

'But I can't act,' Neville insisted, his face turning white at the thought of being onstage again. 'I was only a sheep before. I told you that right from the start.'

'I DON'T CARE!' Rubella screamed. 'I'M A TURNIP BECAUSE OF YOU!'

Off to Rehearsals

BAAAAAAAAAAAAAAAAAAAAAAAAAAAAAANG!

The ticker-dinger-thinger shook the house. Neville opened one eye and stretched. For one tiny blissful moment he'd forgotten where he was and –

'AARGH!' Neville screamed suddenly as Rubella grabbed his ankle and dragged him out of her laundry pile.

'Morning, you pookery little dungle droppin',' she said flatly. 'I can't wait to see what squibbly things you'll be doin' onstage today. Just think – Nev in front of hundreds and hundreds of trolls.'

'NO!' Neville whimpered. 'Get off!'

Rubella swung Neville into the air and caught him under her arm like someone carrying a plank of wood.

'LET ME GO, RUBELLA!'

'Shut up, snot,' she barked. 'You're going to have an absolunkly squibbly day at the theatre with winky ole me.' Then she smiled a frightening smile and stormed down the stairs with Neville still tucked under her arm.

'Mornin', my actory types,' Malaria said as Rubella reached the bottom step. Neville was flailing wildly, kicking and poking his troll-sister in her mammoth behind. He flailed so hard that one of his slippers flew off and landed in Malaria's cooking pot with a *SPLOOSH*.

'Oooh!' Malaria chortled. 'Thanks, Nev. That'll make it taste delunktious. Who's for a spot of something tummy-tinklin'?'

'NO!' Rubella barked as she clomped across the kitchen.

'What about you, Nev?'

'HE'S NOT HUNGRY,' Rubella shot back at her mooma and pushed through the green curtain.

'PLEASE, RUBELLA,' Neville pleaded. 'PUT ME DOWN.'

'SHUT UP!' She gave Neville a warning squeeze and he made a sound like a deflated bagpipe.

'*HOOOOOOOOF!*'

Rubella burst out laughing. 'Maybe you could be an instrument in the band,' she teased.

'*HOOOOOOOOF!*' Neville wheezed. 'STOP IT RU– *OOOOOOOF!* LET ME GO – *OOOOOOOF!* I'M GOING TO BE S– *OOOOOOOF!*'

'Hmmm,' Rubella sighed contentedly. 'This will be more fun than I thought.' With that, she lumbered off towards the theatre, playing Neville like a human one-man band.

'*HOOOOOOOOF!*'

Tonight is the Night!

When they reached the theatre it was bustling with trolls preparing for the show. Rubella dumped Neville on the ground by the front door and stormed inside.

'I'm goin' to find Thicket,' she barked over her shoulder. 'Go and make yourself useful, worm.'

Neville wriggled to his feet and dusted himself off. He felt sick with nerves – and from being squeezed like a human-sized accordion. What was he going to do? He closed his eyes and thought of Captain Brilliant.

'Eww.'

Neville opened his eyes again with a start.

'Eww, it's you.' Gruntilda came out through the front doors wearing an unfinished ballgown made from bed sheets. 'I remember that 'orrible face. You're the overling that lives with the . . . Bulches.' She said 'Bulches' like it was a rude word.

'I'm Neville,' said Neville. He puffed up his chest and tried to look brave.

'You're so ugly,' Gruntilda sneered, poking Neville with her skinny finger to check that he was real. 'Even uglier than that sister of yours.'

'No, I'm not . . . BUT YOU ARE!' retorted Neville bravely.

'I'M NOT! I CAN'T BE UGLY! I'M THE GRUMPTIOUS STEPSISTER!' Gruntilda shouted. 'YOU'RE A BULCH . . . DISGUSTIN'! YOU CAN'T BE IN MY MOOMA'S PAN-TROLL-MIME. YOU'LL RUIN IT!'

'Pardon?' Neville said. Had he heard correctly?

'EVERYONE WILL BE BLURTY IF THEY WATCH YOU ONSTAGE. I'M GOIN' TO TELL MY MOOMSIE AND SHE WON'T LET YOU BE IN THE PAN-TROLL-MIME.'

Neville almost burst out laughing with joy.

He didn't care if that stupid bundle of bones thought he was ugly.

'Oh, please let me be in the show,' Neville lied. He clasped his hands together to make it look really convincing. 'I *really* want to be in it . . . I just have to be . . . it'll make me *SOOOOO* happy. I'll *die* if I don't get to perform.'

'NO!' Gruntilda said with spiteful glee. 'You'll *never* be in it now.'

She grabbed hold of Neville's hand and pulled him towards the doors of the theatre.

'You're goin' to regret this, you ugly, winky overling,' Gruntilda hissed, completely unaware that Neville was grinning behind her. 'Now, come with me.'

Neville followed Gruntilda into the theatre and gasped when he saw the commotion.

There were trolls everywhere. Some were clambering over high scaffolding, hanging extra milk-bottle lanterns, while others were painting huge cloths. One scene showed a strange, exotic landscape made from junk, and another was of the ballroom of a faraway troll-castle.

The troll-band was practising in the priddling pit and Mucus was on the stage with a team of very cumbersome, tutu-ed ballerinas, clapping out a rhythm as they twirled and jumped noisily.

'One, two, three, four, bad toes, pointy toes!' he shouted. 'One, two, three . . . Nettle! Get those legs higher or you're not in the show!'

The young troll named Nettle nodded enthusiastically and kicked her leg as high as it would go. Her overstretched tights ripped loudly and echoed round the theatre. Neville smiled to himself as the other trolls fell about laughing and Mucus stormed offstage, fluttering his grey-green hands and wailing, 'I CAN'T WORK WITH THESE AMATROLLS!'

Neville suddenly felt a tingle of excitement – if he didn't have to be onstage, a pan-troll-mime might be fun to watch!

Meanwhile, a pack of hefty troll-men in black rolled an enormous coach made from hundreds of hammered-together bits of clock on to the stage and positioned it in a pool of light.

'That's the coach Rubella is going to turn into,' said Neville. 'She's the turnip.'

'Ha!' Gruntilda scoffed as she pulled him up the steps and on to the stage. 'Don't mention that name to me . . . Moomsie said she got the lowest score of every troll that auditioned.'

Neville grimaced to himself and hoped Rubella wouldn't find out. She'd be crushed and would probably crush him in return if she did. 'She wasn't that bad,' he said loyally.

'BAD?' Gruntilda laughed. 'Moomsie said she was *disgusterous*.'

Neville stuck his tongue out at Gruntilda's back.

'Moomsie?' Gruntilda said as they approached Abominatia. 'Moomsie?'

Abominatia wasn't listening. She stood there, gnarled hands on hips, shouting at something near the ceiling.

'*DAINTY*, GRISTLE,' she yelled. 'You've got to be more dainty or my show will be ruined.'

Neville looked up just in time to dive out of the way as Gristle Pilchard whizzed past, dangling on the end of a long rope. She was wearing a sparkly dress, covered in milk-bottle tops, and had little wings made from stained paper plates on her back.

'LIKE THIS?' Gristle shouted, flapping her arms up and down like a bird. In one hand she held a magic wand made from a broom handle, with a cardboard star on the top, and she thrashed her walking stick back and forth with the other.

'I really don't think you need your walkin' stick, Gristle,' Abominatia shouted as the old fairy swung back the other way.

'I CAN'T WALK WITHOUT IT, DEARY!'

'YOU DON'T NEED TO WALK, YOU'RE IN THE AIR!' Abominatia's flytrap hair started twitching with frustration.

'Erm . . . Moomsie,' Gruntilda mumbled nervously.

'WHAT?' Abominatia glared at her daughter and pouted.

'Well,' Gruntilda said, ducking as Gristle Pilchard came back for another swing. 'I was just telling this . . . thing –'

'I'm Neville,' Neville interrupted.

'*Ugh!*' Abominatia jolted when she saw him as if he was a nasty surprise. 'You're ugly.' She leaned in for a closer look.

'I'm not ugly, I'm an overling,' Neville snapped.

'I was just tellin' Neville that Rubella Bulch was absolunkly gripeous at the auditions . . . wasn't she.'

Abominatia clutched her throat as if she was about to be sick.

'I can't chattywag about it now,' she said, tossing her shoulder ivy. 'The memory of it is too upsetly.'

'Anyway,' said Gruntilda, sidling wickedly next to her mooma and leering at Neville. 'He called me ugly and I don't want him in the show.'

'YOU CALLED MY DAUGHTER WHAT?'

'I called her really, really ugly,' Neville said with his fingers crossed behind his back. 'But I also really want to perform.'

'NEVER!' Abominatia yelled. 'You will *never* be in the show.'

Inside, Neville felt like bursting into happy tears. Now it didn't matter what Rubella said, he couldn't be in the pan-troll-mime no matter what. He felt so squibbly he could –

'We'll find him another job to do instead,' said Abominatia.

Neville's heart jumped up into his throat.

'What?'

'It's all grabbers on deck,' Abominatia said, flourishing her twiggy arms. 'We'll find you another job.' She called to one of the hefty trolls fixing a wheel on the coach and he plodded over immediately, nodding happily.

'What seems to be the troublin', Miss Bunt?'

Abominatia pointed at Neville. 'This thing –'

'MY NAME IS NEVILLE.'

'Neville,' said Abominatia, gesturing at the other

troll, 'this is Dunk . . . He's in charge of all the technicky-ratchety-doo-dah stuff.'

Neville smiled nervously. The troll had tools and contraptions all over him. There were old rusty spanners and hammers sticking out of every pocket and belt loop. He even had a full set of pliers and hundreds of nuts and bolts knotted up in his grassy hair.

'Dunk, we need to find a job for Neville,' Abominatia ordered. 'He called my daughter ugly, so make it a toughly one.'

'Hmmm!' Dunk looked at Neville as if he was the bravest thing he'd ever seen. 'Well . . . um . . .' Dunk scratched his tool-covered head and thought for a moment. Neville's knees started to tremble.

'Well . . . the hinkapoot trainer needs some help gettin' 'em ready,' the troll said. 'They can be a winky bit tricksy.'

'Perfect,' Abominatia cooed. 'You, Neville, will help our hinkapoots to look razzly and showish.'

'What's a hinkapoot?' asked Neville, his mind filling with dread.

'The overling is a nogginknocker,' Abominatia huffed. 'Every pan-troll-mime always has a team of teensy hinkapoots doin' tricks. It wouldn't be complete without them.'

'Oh,' said Neville. He thought about it for a moment. Maybe playing with hinkapoots would be fun. It had to be better than going onstage. 'I'm quite good at looking after my dog, Napoleon.'

'A *dog*?' Gruntilda blurted.

'What's wrong with you?' Abominatia gasped. 'Hinkapoots are nothin' like dogs. Now wiffle off and help out . . . there isn't much time and everythin' has to be perfect.'

'How long have I got?' Neville asked.

'This is pan-troll-mime,' Abominatia proclaimed, looking dramatically at the ceiling. 'With my artsy vision, we don't waste our time with rehearsals . . . WE OPEN TONIGHT WHEN THE TICKER-DINGER-THINGER GOES *BONG!*'

Neville's jaw dropped open. *Tonight?* The show would be a complete shambles.

'Full cast meetin' as soon as they've fixed the

blunkin' coach wheels. Now off you go!'

Dunk placed a hand on Neville's shoulder and turned to lead him away.

'And, Neville . . .' Abominatia said in a raspy whisper. She slunk over, grabbed Neville by the collar of his pyjamas and pulled him in close. '*I've got my peepers on you.*'

Halitosis and her Amazing Hinka-Circus

Dunk led Neville along a hallway behind the stage. There were dressing rooms on either side with the actors' names painted sloppily on each door and the occasional poster of past shows. Neville read each one as he shuffled past.

MOOMA-MIA
SINGIN' IN THE DRAIN
TROLLEO AND JUBLIET
TROLIVER
WAR AND PIES

Dunk stopped outside the door at the far end of the hallway. The painted sign on it read: HALITOSIS AND HER AMAZING HINKA-CIRCUS.

Neville smiled; that sounded quite fun.

''Ere we are then,' Dunk said, nodding politely. 'Just go in . . . She won't hear if you knock.' Then the hefty troll turned and trudged off back towards the stage, whistling to himself.

'Thanks,' Neville called.

'Ain't no nevermind,' Dunk called back.

Neville waited for a moment, then stepped up to the door and listened. Inside, he could hear a huge commotion clattering about. *Oh no*, he thought. Neville had never actually seen a hinkapoot before. He remembered his mooma describing them as scrawny and little, but that didn't stop them from having massive claws and razor-sharp teeth.

Ignoring what Dunk had said, Neville knocked softly on the door and waited. There was no answer, just the sound of something smashing.

'GET DOWN FROM THERE!' a troll-lady's voice on the other side of the door screamed. 'NO! DON'T EAT THAT!'

Why was everything so scary in the Underneath? Neville braced himself and thought of Captain Brilliant, then grabbed hold of the rusty old doorknob and twisted it.

'Hello,' he said in a pathetic whimper as he pushed the door slightly. 'Hello–*oooooooooooaaaaaaa-gggghhhhh*!!!!'

Something small and green skittered round the surface of the door and jumped on to Neville's face. He ran flailing into the room as the small thing gripped hold of both his ears and held on tight. Neville could feel the pinch of tiny dull teeth trying to bite the end of his nose.

'HELP!' he shrieked, but the second he opened his mouth, a small foot wedged itself in there. '*HMELPH!*'

'OH, MY GRACICLES!' The troll-lady's voice gasped. 'HOLD STILL!'

Neville didn't dare open his eyes. The thing on his face started chittering and squeaking wildly as a pair of troll-hands reached up and scooped it off.

'Grimble, that's not nice . . . Naughty Grimble.'

Neville stood there, frozen in horror, with his eyes clamped shut.

'It's OK,' said the voice. 'You can look now.'

Neville wasn't sure he wanted to.

'Really,' she said. 'I've got him; he won't jump on you again.'

Neville very carefully opened one eye and peeked at the troll before him. She was a round troll-girl with palm leaves for hair and large magnifying-glass spectacles.

'Hello,' she said, and smiled a shy smile. 'I'm Halitosis. Sorry about him.' She held the hinkapoot out at arm's length for Neville to see.

'I'm Neville,' said Neville, gawping at the odd green thing struggling in Halitosis's hands. It was wearing a little collar with a tag that read GRIMBLE. 'Abominatia sent me.'

'Oh, squibbly,' Halitosis said. She gently put Grimble down on the floor and did a funny hand gesture like the dog trainers at Napoleon's puppy classes. 'STAY!'

Neville couldn't help but stare. The hinkapoot was the strangest thing he'd ever seen – a kind of cross between a troll and lots of types of animals. It was about as high as Neville's knee and was covered from head to toe in light green and dark green stripes. It had a long body with little hands, feet and a face just like a miniature troll, but out of the top of its head popped a set of enormous rabbit-like ears.

'*CHEE-CHIK-BUHH-BRAA-CHIK!*' it hollered in a tiny voice.

'OH!' Neville yelped. 'It's um . . .'

'He can be a bit rampageous sometimes,' said Halitosis. 'But he's very friendly. Grimble just thought you were food, didn't you, Grimble?'

The little thing looked at Neville and licked its lips.

'They eat anythin',' Halitosis said, giggling.

'Oh, b-brilliant,' Neville stammered. He squirmed and backed away, only to hear more chittering right by his ear.

'*CHIK-CHI-CHI-CHIK!*'

'ARGH!' Neville spun round to see another hinkapoot hanging off a set of coat pegs, waggling its ears at him. 'EWW!' He spun back to Halitosis and realized, with growing nervousness, that the room was crawling with hinkapoots. They were sitting on the top of an old wardrobe and crawling over the floor and walls. One was even swinging on a milk-bottle lantern above Neville's head.

'*CHIK-CHUH-GRA-BRIK-BRIK!*' they all chirped together. Neville almost jumped out of his pyjamas with surprise.

'Don't get jangled,' said Halitosis reassuringly. She picked up a cane from a broken table and knocked it three times on the floor. The hinkapoots instantly jumped into formation and created a hinkapoot pyramid with Grimble at the top. 'I have all of them under control.'

'Ha!' Neville chuckled, suddenly mesmerized by the little creatures. 'I can see that.'

'Now,' said Halitosis in a big voice, 'let's show

Neville what you can do.'

She tapped three more times on the floor and the hinkapoots darted about, spinning cartwheels and leapfrogging over one another. Then they formed a circle round Neville's feet and did flips in both directions.

'They're amazing,' said Neville, desperately trying to ignore the urge to cringe.

'Thanks.' Halitosis scuffed her feet shyly. 'So . . . um . . . why did Abominatia send you?'

'Oh, I'm supposed to help you get the hinkapoots ready. They're starting soon.'

Panic spread across Halitosis's face as if she'd been slapped by an invisible hand.

'NOW?' she barked. 'OH, POOK! *NOW?*'

'Yes, I think so,' said Neville. 'Why, what's

wrong? They look ready to go, if you ask me.'

'We have to get them dressed . . . QUICK!' Halitosis shrieked. 'If we're late, Abominatia will explode. She's crazy.'

Halitosis dashed to the wardrobe and started pulling out armfuls of tiny, hinkapoot-sized clothing.

'What do you think?' she said, holding up two different types of outfit. 'Ruffly or not ruffly?'

'Erm.' Neville didn't know what to say. He didn't have a clue what kind of clothes looked good on a hinkapoot. 'Ruffly?'

'Good choice,' said Halitosis. She threw a bunch of ruffles to Neville and grabbed some for herself. 'All we have to do is get them on.'

'What do I have to do?' said Neville.

Halitosis gave Neville a playful look and shouted, '*CHARGE!*'

Without stopping to think, Neville copied Halitosis and grabbed a hinkapoot off the wall. It wriggled in his hands and *CHIK-CHIK*-ed angrily.

'Like this,' Halitosis said, showing Neville how to smooth down the hinkapoot's ears and slide the

little ruffled collar over its head. 'Just show it who's boss.' She then took the dressed little creature and dropped it into a big wicker hamper.

'OK,' Neville said. His heart was beating fast. Dressing hinkapoots was fun and dangerous all in one go and made him feel a bit like his hero, Captain Brilliant. '*CHARGE!*'

Halitosis and Neville jumped about the room, grabbing hinkapoots from all directions.

'THERE!'

'GOT ONE!'

'BEHIND YOU!'

One by one the hinkapoots were dressed and deposited in the basket. They wriggled and chirped inside, but the lid stayed put and none escaped, to Neville's relief.

'All done,' Halitosis said with a big grin. 'I'm so excited. They're goin' to try a new trick tonight.'

'What's the trick?' asked Neville, rubbing a stinging hinka-bite on his knuckle.

'It's never been performed before in all the history of hinka-circuses,' Halitosis said. She wriggled her fingers as if she was casting a magic spell. 'The Tremundous Hinka-hurl.'

'What's that?'

'Every hinkapoot stands on the next one's shoulders until they're all in a big tower. Then Grimble climbs to the top and they throw him as high as he can go . . . Higher than any hinkapoot's gone before.'

'Wow,' Neville said. His nerves were slowly creeping away and he was starting to feel genuinely excited about the show. He only wished he could sit in the theatre and watch it.

Halitosis grabbed hold of one of the basket handles and nodded to indicate that Neville should grab the other.

'It's showtime,' she said.

They were just in time. As Neville opened the dressing-room door and started pulling the basket up the hall, the ticker-dinger-thinger went . . .

BOOOOONNNNGGGG!!!

Meanwhile

'LAST CHANCE . . . AGAIN!' Abominatia growled. She poked her twig-like finger into the end of Gruntilda's nose and scowled. 'SING IT AGAIN AND THIS TIME SING THE RIGHT NOTES, YOU SKWARKER!'

'I *did* sing the right notes,' Gruntilda whined. 'Everyone knows I've got a voice like a chooney-chuff. That's why I got the part of the grumptious stepsister.'

'If you ever want to be as hoop-di-doo-cious as your moomsie, sing it again,' Abominatia shouted. She whacked Gruntilda on the top of her head, making her branchy hair creak. 'After all, Moomsie knows best.'

'*Ow*,' Gruntilda moaned, then instantly started singing her love song for the show.

'That's better,' said Abominatia with a vinegary

smile. Then she turned away and grimaced. The sound of her daughter screeching was unbearable.

PLACES!

Neville and Halitosis heaved the basket into the wings of the stage and panted. Hinkapoots were heavier than they looked.

'That's squibbly,' Halitosis said to Neville. 'Thanks.'

'I can't wait to see them do their trick,' Neville said.

'I know!' Halitosis laughed, pulling a nervous face. 'It's right at the end. Don't miss it.'

'Promise,' Neville said.

With that Halitosis ambled off, leaving Neville to have a look around.

A lot of the acty-trolls were already gathered on the stage, warming up, as Neville wandered out. He soon began to enjoy the sensation of being unseen behind the front curtain and hearing the audience chattering excitedly and the band rehearsing on the other side. This was going to be fun.

Thicket was doing squats in the corner and flexing his bulging arms. He was wearing a cape made from an old bath towel, with holes for his thorn briars, and a dented crown on his head made from old bent keys.

'Grotsome,' he said, winking and smiling at the girl dancers as they giggled past. 'Totally grotsome.'

Neville rolled his eyes and turned away. Where had Rubella got to?

'Magicky, spookery, trickedy!' Gristle Pilchard

was still dangling on the end of a rope, practising her lines and waving both her wand and her walking stick. Neville looked at her curiously. In addition to her sparkly dress and wings, she'd stuck on a tufty wig and a long curly beard.

'Why does she have a beard?' Neville asked Dunk as he trudged by. The technicky-ratchety-doo-dah-troll looked at Neville as if it was the most stupid question ever.

'She's the furry bog-mother,' said Dunk. 'She's got to be furry.'

Neville nodded and laughed. 'Of course.'

'Anyway, it's nearly showtime, Nev,' Dunk said. ''Elp a troll out and straighten that cloth, will ya? It's all wonksome.'

Neville looked to where Dunk was pointing. He was right. The massive cloth painted like a troll ballroom had a huge bulge in the middle of it.

'No problem, Dunk,' Neville said. He felt extremely grown-up and brave, doing jobs for the technicky-troll. 'Won't be a minute.'

Walking over to the cloth, Neville gave the bulge a great big push to try and flatten it out.

'OY!' came Rubella's voice. 'BUNGLE OFF!'

'Oh, Rubella,' Neville yelped. 'Is that you?' He bent down and wriggled underneath. 'I was wondering where you'd got to.'

'NO, DON'T COME UNDER!' ordered Rubella. 'YOU MUSTN'T –'

It was too late. Neville squirmed under the heavy cloth and gasped. Rubella was wearing her turnip costume and a very unhappy scowl on her face.

'You look . . . um . . .'

'*I look like a blunkin' nogginknocker!*' Rubella bellowed. She was wearing a huge round ball with holes for her hands and feet. It had been painted to look like the rough purple skin of a turnip and even had little roots drooping down between her chubby ankles.

'I was going to say "squibbly",' said Neville, desperately trying not to laugh at her little hat with green leaves sprouting out of it.

'*I hate you!*' Rubella sobbed. She attempted to smack Neville across his head, but couldn't reach because of the armholes. 'AAAAAARGH!'

'MY DUNKLINGS!'

The stage went silent. Neville grabbed Rubella's hand and pulled her out from behind the scenery cloth. Everyone was staring at Abominatia as she walked on to the stage with Gruntilda trailing behind in her bed-sheet ballgown. The bony girl took one look at Rubella and snickered.

'IT IS TIME!' Abominatia announced. 'I'M SURE YOU'LL ALL BE WONDERBUNKIN' AND AMAZEROUS . . .'

Everyone smiled and nodded.

'AND IF YOU'RE NOT . . .'

Everyone stopped smiling.

'I'LL KILL YOU!'

Everyone looked worried. Very worried.

'PLACES, PEOPLE! OPENIN' POSITIONS! *GO!*'

Meanwhile

'I'm so exciterous, I think I might burst my barnacles,' Clod said, taking his seat next to Malaria and Pong with an armful of food from the snackety stand. The theatre was packed. 'I honk pan-troll-mimes, I do.'

Clod grinned at Pong, who was wearing a little version of his dooda's trollabaloo suit and waving a paper *WHINGERELLA* flag.

'Calm yourself down, my brandyburp.' Malaria chuckled and planted a kiss on Clod's cheek. 'It ain't even started yet.'

'I can't 'elp it,' said Clod. 'It's just so spectactical.'

Suddenly, the lights dimmed as the technicky-trolls extinguished the milk-bottle lanterns and the band started to play a jiggish tune. Everyone in the audience cheered and whooped.

It Begins

Backstage, everyone was in position. Neville stood next to Dunk at the side of the stage and felt butterflies in his belly.

'Just do everything I say, and it'll all be fine and peachous,' Dunk whispered.

This is it, thought Neville. He scrunched up his toes and pulled on the rope that Dunk had pointed out to him moments before. As if by magic, the front curtain rose to reveal an enormous painted cloth of rolling hills of junk. The old troll Bowel stood out in front, coughing and scratching his toadstools nervously.

The audience *ooooh*-ed and *aaaah*-ed as Bowel took a big step forward, waved and smiled a toothy grin. Then he began to sing.

'MOOMAS AND DOODAS, LITTLE LUMPS
AND OLDY TROLLS AS WELL.
HAVE A SEAT, PRICK UP YOUR EARS.
WE'VE GOT A TALE TO TELL.'

Bowel swayed from side to side as he sang, and the audience clapped wildly.

'IN A JUNKISH LAND, SO FAR AWAY,
LIVED A GRUNT CALLED WHINGERELLA,
AND HER GRUMPTIOUS HONKIN' STEPSISTER
AND A DASHLY PRINCEY FELLA.'

Suddenly, the audience booed and hissed. Dunk turned a handle on the wall and something rose out of a trapdoor in the stage. It was an upside-down mop with a dress on it like a person.

'*BOOOOOOO . . . HISSSSSSSS . . . BOOOOOOO!*'

Neville laughed to himself. Rubella wasn't lying when she said no one liked Whingerella. No actor would even play her.

Bowel gestured to the mop-Whingerella.

'OLE WHINGEY HAD A STEPSISTER,
TOO GRUMPTIOUS TO DO CHORES,
LIKE MOPPIN', FOLDIN', BREWIN' TEA
AND LICKIN' CLEAN THE FLOORS.'

Gruntilda walked out onstage and fanned herself daintily.

'It's so hard being this good-looksy.' She sighed and batted her eyelashes.

'ALL DAY WHINGEY GRIZZLY-GRIPED
AND SAT ON HER BEHIND.
WHILE HER RAVISHLY HELPY SISTER
WAS WONDERBUNKLY KIND.'

The audience *ahhh*-ed the grumptious stepsister until Gruntilda stepped forward and started to sing.

'WHERE, OH WHERE IS MY WARTY PRINCE?' Gruntilda screeched at the crowd. Everyone groaned and covered their ears. 'WON'T HE COME TO ME?'

'NOT LIKELY,' a troll in the crowd shouted and the audience burst out laughing.

Backstage, Neville pulled the rope that changed the scenery from the rolling junk hills to Whingerella's kitchen. He turned round and saw Rubella glowering at him in the dark.

'I don't want to do this,' she hissed.

'You can't back out now, Rubella,' Neville said. 'Besides, do you want Gruntilda to think she's beaten you?'

'No,' Rubella said miserably, and straightened her turnip hat.

'ONE NIGHT THE GRUMPTIOUS STEPSISTER
WAS SWOONIN' AND A REELIN'
WHEN – *CRASH!* – THE FURRY BOG-MOTHER
CAME FLYIN' THROUGH THE CEILIN'.'

Bowel presented an arm to the top of the stage and waited. He gestured again, but nothing happened. An awkward silence filled the theatre.

'CAME FLYIN' THROUGH THE CEILIN'!' Bowel shouted again.

A sparkly shoe covered in milk-bottle tops fell from somewhere above the stage and bounced off Bowel's head with a dull thud.

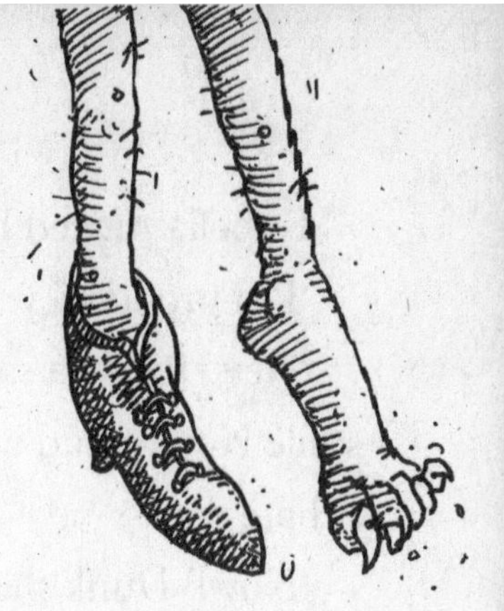

'CAME FLYIN' THROUGH THE CEILIN',' Bowel bellowed at the top of his voice.

'Oooh!' a little voice shouted from high in the air. 'IS IT ME, DEARLY?'

All at once, Gristle Pilchard came plummeting down through the air and swung so fast across the stage that she vanished into the side-curtains like a geriatric rocket. The audience roared with laughter at the sight of her feet waggling in the air wearing only one shoe.

And so it went on.

Eventually, it was Rubella's turn.

'Rubella,' Neville whispered. 'It's time.'

Rubella waddled miserably into place behind the kitchen scenery cloth and did her best turnip pose.

'Stand by,' Dunk whispered from the other side of the stage.

Neville looked at his troll-sister in her turnip costume and suddenly felt very sorry for her.

'Rubella,' Neville said quietly.

Rubella turned her head and looked at him.
'I'm proud of you.'
'Nev,' Rubella said back. She smiled the sweetest smile Neville had ever seen his sister manage. 'I hate you.'
'Now!' Dunk shouted.
Neville pulled on a rope and the kitchen scenery cloth flew out, revealing a junk-filled garden complete with a very oversized turnip.

'THERE SHE IS!' Clod shouted, rocking back and forth in his seat. 'MY BELLY, ALL BIG AND JUBBLY AND TURNIPY.'

'I'm proud plonkless,' Malaria said, wiping a tear away.

Backstage, Neville and Halitosis were getting the hinkapoots ready for their first entrance. He watched as Halitosis opened the basket lid and did one of her funny hand gestures, making all the hinkapoots stand very still.

'All righty,' she said to the little green creatures. 'To the coach.'

The hinkapoots quickly clambered out of the basket and ran to the front of the clock-coach that stood a little way away in the dark. They grabbed hold of the ropes that dangled from the front of it and waited silently for Halitosis's command.

Onstage, Gristle Pilchard was finally out of the curtain and flapping gracefully above Gruntilda.

'BRING ME A TURNIP,' Gristle cried, 'AND EVERY COCK-A-ROACH.'

Rubella waddled over to the centre of the stage and did a little twirl.

'TURNIP!' she shouted.

'AND WITH MY MAGIC SPELLS,' yelled

Gristle, 'YOU'LL HAVE A HINKAPOOT-DRAWN COACH!'

Bowel pointed to the back of the theatre and bellowed, 'GOOD GRACICLES! . . . LOOK OVER THERE!'

The audience turned round and looked in the direction of Bowel's stumpy finger as Rubella darted offstage as fast as her turnip feet could carry her, and the hinkapoots quickly pulled on the coach made from bits of clock.

The audience turned back round and gasped.

'IT'S MAGIC,' cried Clod. 'ABSOLUNKLY MAGICOUS!'

The Hinka-Hamper

After pulling Gruntilda round in the coach and waiting for the troll-ball scenery cloth to lower in front of them, the hinkapoots all skittered back to the side of the stage and gathered round Halitosis's feet.

'Congruntulations,' she whispered to them. 'You were marvellish.'

'That was great,' Neville said to Halitosis.

'Thanks!' The troll-girl beamed. 'Listen, Nev, I have to glump back to the dressin' room and get some things readsy for the Tremundous Hinka-hurl. Can you get them back in the basket and lock the lid for me?'

'No problem,' said Neville.

'Squibbly!'

Halitosis walked away, leaving Neville with the little crowd of hinkapoots. He carefully lifted the lid of the hamper and pointed inside.

'IN!' he said, trying to sound as commanding as possible.

Nothing happened.

'IN!' Neville said again.

The hinkapoots stared at him with their tiny jet-black eyes and . . . and . . . *OH NO!*

The hinkapoots scattered in all directions.

'COME BACK!' Neville howled as they shimmied up the curtains and spun around the floor. He tried to grab them as fast as he could and fling them into the basket. 'Please don't go on the stage . . . PLEASE DON'T GO ON THE STAGE!'

'*CHIK-CHI-BRUK-BRUH-CHIK!*'

'*Ouch!*' Neville pulled one off his leg as it bit his knee, and grabbed another three that were swinging on the scenery ropes. He had to jump to catch one that was scampering up the hallway doorframe, and then tug at another that was chewing the spokes on the back wheels of the coach. This was terrible!

Huffing and puffing, Neville dropped the little beasts into the basket and counted them.

'One, two, three, four, five, six, seven, eight,

nine . . .' Neville was sure there had been ten hinkapoots before. He started looking frantically about. Halitosis would be so upset if one of her hinkapoots was missing and they weren't able to perform the Tremundous Hinka-hurl.

'Hello,' he whispered. 'Little hinka–'

Neville froze. There in the doorway that led to the dressing rooms stood the tenth and final hinkapoot. It waggled its ears and chirped happily. Neville noticed the little tag dangling round the creature's neck and his heart started racing even faster. It was Grimble, Halitosis's prize hinkapoot.

'*CLICK-CHIK-CHRUP-CHIK-CHIK!*'

Grimble stuck its little green tongue out at Neville, then turned and bounded down the hallway.

Meanwhile

Abominatia sat brooding in her own private director's dressing room, drumming her fingers on the table.

'*Guh!*' she huffed. Had she definitely made sure that no one knew the truth about Gruntilda? All of a sudden, Abominatia couldn't remember what she'd done with the torn-up scorecard and it worried her in the pit of her stomach. *What if . . . ?*

Just then she heard a rustling coming from the storeroom next door – and suddenly remembered where she'd stuffed the card.

Abominatia rose slowly from her seat and sniffed the air.

'Overling,' she grunted.

Something wasn't right . . .

Discovered

'Grimble?' Neville said, quietly tiptoeing into the storeroom. 'Come out now.'

Neville felt helpless. He looked around at the shadowy piles of junk and boxes of costumes and felt his heart sink. What was he going to do? He felt sure he'd seen the little green thing scamper in here, but it could be hiding under anything by now. It would take hours to dig the pesky hinkapoot out.

'Grimble, it's me . . . Come out now,' Neville whispered.

He was just walking round a stack of old troll-sized top hats that went all the way up to the ceiling, when a flash of green shot out from under a chair and darted up the wall. It stopped in the top corner and turned to look at Neville, waggling its rabbit-like ears.

'Oh, there you are,' Neville said, smiling and trying to look as inviting as possible. 'Erm . . . we can play games if you come down.'

'*CHI-CHI-CHI-CHI-CHI-CHIK!*' Grimble gnashed his little teeth and scowled.

'OK.' Neville edged a little closer. 'Maybe I can find you . . . um . . . a snack?'

'*GRUH-GU-GAH!*' Grimble squeaked and scrambled towards him.

'Oh . . . ha! OK, you're hungry . . . um . . .' Neville looked about for something to feed to the hinkapoot. Halitosis had said they ate almost anything, so it couldn't be too hard to find something to tempt the little creature.

'Aha!' Neville noticed two pieces of card sticking out of an old box of costumes. Maybe that would be enough. 'It's tasty,' Neville said, grabbing the pieces and waving them at arm's length. 'It's very, very –'

Neville stopped. He noticed the words Rubella Bulch were scrawled across the top of one of them.

Forgetting about Grimble for a moment, Neville moved closer to the light pouring in from the hallway. He put the two ripped edges together and read what was on them.

Neville's jaw dropped open. It was the scorecard from the pan-troll-mime auditions! *Rubella had won the part of the grumptious stepsister fair and square and someone had lied about it.*

'I HAVE TO TELL RUBELLA!' Neville said to himself. He stuffed the pieces of card into his pocket, spun on his heel and cried out loud in shock. The doorway was filled with a very tall, very angry troll-woman with twitching, flytrap hair.

Abominatia's Secret

'Just where do you think you're wifflin' off to, you . . . you skunkus little lump of foozle fodder?' Abominatia hissed, edging menacingly into the storeroom.

'Erm . . . I-I was just looking for a missing h-hinkapoot,' Neville stammered. 'That's all . . . I should be getting back to the stage . . . Dunk will be needing me.' He tried to walk round Abominatia, but she seized him by the scruff of his collar and bowled him back into the room. Neville stumbled against the high tower of hats, nearly knocking it over.

'I DON'T THINK SO!' she screamed. 'I KNOW YOU SAW THE SCORECARD!'

'Scorecard?' Neville laughed uneasily. 'What scorecard?'

'SHUT UP, YOU GRUBLING!' Abominatia's

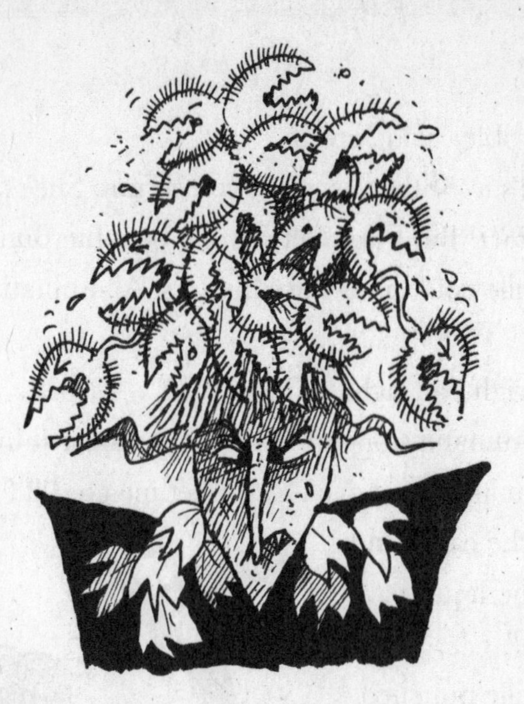

flytrap hair started to writhe and gnash. 'SO WHAT DO YOU PLAN TO DO, NEV?'

'Well . . .' Neville decided not to be scared. He planted his feet wide, gritted his teeth and thought of Captain Brilliant. 'I'M GOING TO TELL RUBELLA.'

'*Ha!*' Abominatia cackled. 'You actually think I'll let you leave this room alive and ruin generations of showbizzly talentin'? My daughter is amazely!'

'But you cheated.'

'*So what?* I had to . . . my daughter . . . is . . . she . . . is . . .'

'Terrible,' said Neville.

'She's *worse* than terrible, you skrunt. She's *ROTTISH*! But I *won't* let anyone beat the Bunts!'

Neville couldn't believe his ears. Abominatia was insane.

'All right, all right,' Neville said.

Abominatia stopped yelling and stared at him.

'I'll make you a deal. If you let me go, I'll forget about the cards and leave them just . . . HERE!'

Neville punched the tower of hats, sending them raining down on Abominatia. A particularly big hat fell and wedged itself over the mad troll-woman's face. She clutched at it and scrabbled this way and that like a headless chicken, as

Neville scooted round her and darted back up the corridor towards the stage. He'd worry about finding Grimble later.

'COME HERE, YOU DISGUSTEROUS LITTLE WHELP!' Abominatia screamed, tripping over a box of shoes and tumbling to the floor. The hat came off her head with a loud *THWUK.*

'I'LL GET YOU!'

The Secret's Out

Neville sprinted to the stage area and along behind the painted backcloth. He could hear from the band's playing and Gruntilda's awful singing that they were near the end of the show.

He had to find Rubella.

Dashing round a group of troll-ballerinas, Neville found Dunk on the other side of the stage, getting ready to push on a big piece of scenery. He looked up at Neville and shook his head.

'Where you been, Nev?' Dunk asked, looking disappointed. 'I've been lookin' for you.'

'There's no time to explain, Dunk,' Neville wheezed. 'Abominatia's gone mad, she's going to kill me . . . I have to find Rubella.'

'Rubella?' Dunk puzzled, scratching his head as if nothing Neville had just said was shocking. 'Is she the parsnip?'

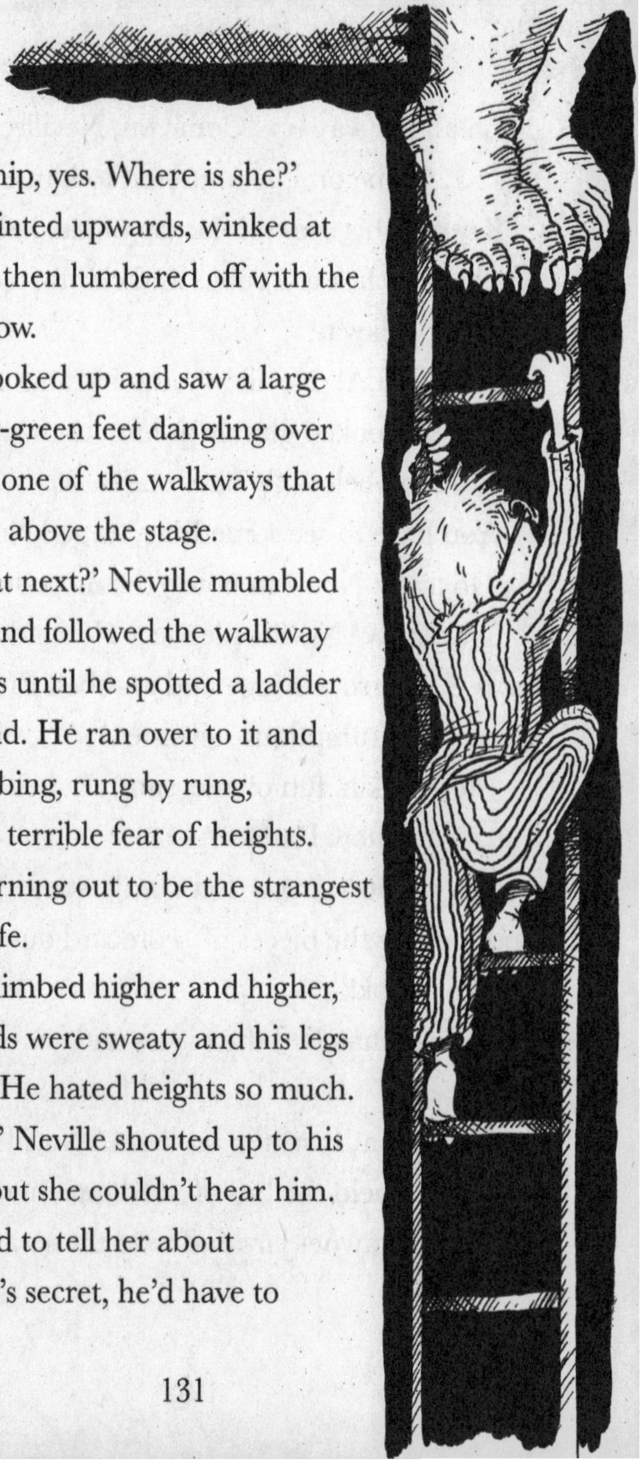

'The turnip, yes. Where is she?'

Dunk pointed upwards, winked at Neville and then lumbered off with the scenery in tow.

Neville looked up and saw a large pair of grey-green feet dangling over the edge of one of the walkways that arched high above the stage.

'Oh, what next?' Neville mumbled to himself and followed the walkway with his eyes until he spotted a ladder at the far end. He ran over to it and started climbing, rung by rung, ignoring his terrible fear of heights. This was turning out to be the strangest day of his life.

Neville climbed higher and higher, but his hands were sweaty and his legs felt wobbly. He hated heights so much.

'Rubella!' Neville shouted up to his troll-sister, but she couldn't hear him. If he wanted to tell her about Abominatia's secret, he'd have to climb all the way up. 'Come on, Neville, you can do this . . . Come on,' he muttered to himself.

Keeping his eyes on the top of the ladder, Neville climbed the last few rungs and clambered on to the wooden walkway.

'RUBELLA!' Neville shouted again.

Rubella looked glumly at him, then looked back at the scene below. 'What?' she said.

'You have to see something,' urged Neville.

'Go away, Nev, I'm not in the moodsie.'

'No, really,' Neville pleaded. He made himself cross the narrow bridge and grabbed Rubella's arm. '*You*'re the grumptious stepsister.'

'Stop makin' fun of me, snot,' Rubella growled at him. 'You know I'm not.'

'No . . . no . . . you don't understand,' Neville said, pulling the pieces of scorecard out of his back pocket. 'Look!'

Rubella snatched the pieces and stared at them. 'What?'

'Look what's written on them,' Neville said.

Rubella held the bits of card together in the light from the scrawnet jars and read the scribbled writing.

'"Rubella Bulch – fifty-three points . . ."
RUBELLA BULCH – FIFTY-THREE POINTS?'
Rubella almost flopped head first off the wooden walkway with surprise. 'WHERE DID YOU FIND THIS?'

'In the old storeroom,' Neville whispered. 'Abominatia knows I've seen it . . . and she's after me.'

'THAT HUMPER!' Rubella barked, puffing out her cheeks. She stood up, slipped off her turnip costume and rolled up the sleeves of her dress beneath it. 'THAT POODLY, PLOPPISH OLD POOK . . . WE'LL SHOW HER NOT TO MESS WITH THE BULCHES . . . AND HER TWIGLING OF A DAUGHTER.'

A smile crept into the corner of Neville's mouth. He looked at Rubella, who winked, picked up a disused sandbag and hurled it down at the stage below.

Meanwhile

Abominatia stalked to the stage area, sniffing the air for the scent of young overling. When she found him, she'd pull him into little pieces and feed him to her flytraps.

'You filthy little worm,' she hissed as she stood there, silently searching the darkness with her copper eyes.

Abominatia was just about to head back and look in the dressing rooms, when a sandbag hurtled down and exploded in a cloud of reddish dust. She looked up and saw two pairs of feet shuffling about through the slats of the walkway above.

'Think you can ruin my pan-troll-mime, Neville?' she whispered, slinking towards the ladder. 'Think again . . .'

Sabotage

'THE PRINCE RODE ALL AROUND THE TOWN,
LEFT AND UP AND RIGHT AND DOWN,
AND WOULD NOT LET A GIRLY PASS
UNTIL SHE TRIED THE SHOE OF GRASS.'

Bowel sang at the top of his voice as Thicket galloped round the stage on a pretend dungle, stopping at various troll-ballerinas and kneeling in front of them with the grumptious stepsister's grass shoe.

'Where can that grumptious honker be?' Thicket exclaimed to the audience. 'I wish she'd come and marry me.'

All of a sudden, Gruntilda appeared through a door in the scenery and ran towards the prince, fluttering her arms.

'Princey-poo, my dunklin' dear,' she shouted in

her scratchy voice. ''Tis I, my honk, 'tis I, I'm here!'

'Grumptious!' Thicket cheered. 'Marry me?'

Gruntilda started flapping towards her honksome prince, when a sandbag suddenly plunged down from above and smashed straight through the stage between them.

CRRAAAAAAAAAASSSSSSSHHHHHHH!!!

'ARGH!' screeched Gruntilda. She looked at Bowel, who shrugged, and then at Thicket. 'What's goin' on?'

The audience started to laugh.

'Shut up, Gruntilda,' Thicket whispered, turning away from the cheering crowd. 'Just say your lines.'

'OH, MY PRINCE,' Gruntilda swooned, giving Thicket a poke in the ribs. 'I'M SO CHUFFLY!'

CRRAAAAAAAAAASSSSSSSHHHHHHH!!!

Another sandbag came soaring down from the rafters.

'I say . . .' Gruntilda chuckled nervously. 'Funny weather, Princey.'

'What are you doin'?' Thicket murmured

through gritted teeth. 'Stop makin' up lines.'

Gruntilda pulled a face at Thicket and turned to the audience. 'What a squibbly day,' she said and pouted.

Bowel walked to the centre of the stage and spread his arms wide.

'THE PRINCE AND HIS GRUMPTIOUS
WERE MARRIED THAT DAY;
THEY JUMPED ON HIS DUNGLE
AND RODE FAR AWAY.'

The mop-Whingerella rose back through the trapdoor and wobbled there next to Bowel.

'BUT DON'T FORGET WHINGEY,
THAT ROTTISH OLD LIZARD.
THE PRINCE KILLED HER DEAD
WITH A JAB TO THE GIZZARD.'

Thicket and Gruntilda galloped past on their pretend dungle and kicked the mop over as they went. The audience cheered and clapped and stamped their feet.

Gruntilda walked to the front to take a bow when –

CRRAAAAAAAAAASSSSSSHHHHHHH!!!

CRRAAAAAAAAAAAAASSSSSSHHHHHHH!!!

CRRAAAAAAAAAAAAAAAASSSSSSSHHHHHH!!!

Up above, Rubella was crying with laughter as she lobbed more and more sandbags over the edge of the walkway.

'Did you see that?' she shouted to Neville. 'HA!'

Neville suddenly felt incredibly naughty – and liked the feeling a lot.

'Watch this,' he said, and pulled on a rope near the wall. All at once, the cloth painted like Whingerella's kitchen was released and came tumbling down on Gruntilda's head, covering her completely.

'Grotsome, Nev!' Rubella laughed.

Neville beamed to himself. No one had ever called him 'grotsome' before.

'WHAT THE . . .?' Gruntilda screamed from under the scenery cloth. She started running about the stage like an oversized, saggy ghost. 'GET ME OUT!'

'What d'ya think, Nev?' Rubella smirked. 'Shall

we let her out?' She pulled on a heavy chain – and another trapdoor opened in the floor. Gruntilda and the scenery cloth flopped into it like laundry down a chute.

'BYE-BYE, BUNTY!' Neville called. He was having so much fun he'd almost forgotten about Abominatia.

'WHAT NOW?' Rubella asked.

'You've got a prince to catch,' Neville said.

'Oh yeah!' Rubella replied with a grin. 'But not before I deal with ole skinny ribs.' Then she dived off the platform, straight down through the trapdoor after Gruntilda.

Neville watched his troll-sister go, then turned to climb down the ladder. But something stopped him in his tracks and he instantly felt a cold sweat break out across the back of his neck.

'*UUUUUURRRRGGGHHHHHH!*'

Abominatia screeched as she tore along the platform towards him with her twiggy claws outstretched.

'*AAAAAIIIIIIEEEEEEEEEEEEGGGHHHHH!*'

Neville tried to duck out of the way, but Abominatia was too fast and she grabbed hold of him. 'I'LL PULL YOUR UGLY LITTLE HEAD OFF!' she screamed. 'I'LL SNAP YOUR – *EEEEEEK!*'

Abominatia tripped on the coil of Gristle's furry bog-mother rope and wobbled towards the edge. Before she could steady herself, she tumbled over the railing and dragged Neville with her.

The Tremundous Hinka-Hurl

Abominatia and Neville plummeted towards the stage, screaming like a pair of banshees.

'GET OFF!' Neville hollered as he saw the ground rushing up to meet them.

'*OH, POOOOOOOOK!*' He scrunched his eyes and braced himself for a painful landing. But –

TWANG-ANG-ANG-ANG!

The rope that Abominatia had tripped on was now caught round her ankle, and the pair swung across the stage just before hitting the floor.

'LET GO!' Neville yelled as he managed to shove two fingers up Abominatia's nostrils and wiggle them around.

'*Puhh!*' she snorted. '*Puhh!*' She thrashed her arms about and suddenly let Neville shoot out of her grip as she scratched at the open air. 'I'M GOIN' TO SPLAT YOU!'

A large, round-shouldered troll in the audience jumped out of her seat, spat out a mouthful of rat patty and bellowed, 'THAT'S MY NEV!'

It was Malaria. She hurdled over the seats in front of her and scrambled towards the stage at breakneck speed. 'I'M COMIN'!'

Neville couldn't focus on anything while spinning through the air. He felt like a rag doll in a washing machine as the lights and the audience and stage and the curtains all whizzed past him again and again.

'I'VE GOT YOU, NEV!' Malaria bounded on to the stage and caught Neville with a grunt. For a moment he thought Abominatia had got him again, until Malaria squeezed him in a big troll-hug and kissed him on the head.

'MOOMA!' Neville shouted. He'd never felt so relieved.

'What's goin' on, Nev?' Malaria asked, putting him down on the floor. 'All this globbergruntin' and all?'

Neville staggered over to where Abominatia was hanging upside down above the stage, growling and scrabbling.

'This is Abominatia Bunt,' Neville shouted to the audience.

'Shut up, you little pile of slurch spit,' she hissed, swiping her arms at Neville.

'Oy!' said Malaria. 'You watch those nasty words or I'll stuff your gobber up with that ivy of yours.'

'Yeah,' Rubella joined in. She suddenly clambered out of the trapdoor wearing Gruntilda's ballgown. The audience cried in alarm. There were rips down the sides and her

gut oozed out like a burst icing bag. 'WHY DON'T YOU TRY PICKIN' ON ME?'

'GET AWAY FROM ME, YOU BULCH!' Abominatia blurted.

'She,' Neville continued, 'is a liar, a cheat and a bully! She hid the audition scorecards and took the part of the grumptious stepsister away from Rubella Bulch.'

The audience gasped.

'BELLY?' Malaria shouted. 'MY BELLY, A PRINCESS?'

'Gonker!' Neville said and pointed at Abominatia.

The audience *umm*-ed and *ooh*-ed.

'NO, I'M NOT . . . I'M AN ARTSY, SHOWBIZZLY BRAINY-BONK AND MY DAUGHTER IS WONDEROUS!'

'You're a fuzzbonk,' came a voice from behind. Everyone turned to see Halitosis step through the curtain with her team of hinkapoots following in a line behind. 'My hinkapoots told me everything . . . YOU'RE A BIG, UGGISH GONKER AND . . . AND . . . YOUR DAUGHTER SINGS LIKE A STRANGLED SLURCH!'

'THAT'S IT!' Abominatia shouted at Halitosis. 'YOU AND YOUR DISGUSTEROUS DANCIN' BOGEYS WILL NEVER WORK IN THIS THEATRE AGAIN . . . THE SAME GOES FOR THE REST OF YOU AS WELL!'

'Who cares?' Dunk growled, stepping on from the other side of the stage. He brandished a large spanner and frowned at Abominatia.

The upside-down troll-lady looked suddenly nervous.

'You always made my life miserous,' added Mucus as he leapt out from behind a curtain, spun, flipped and struck a pose.

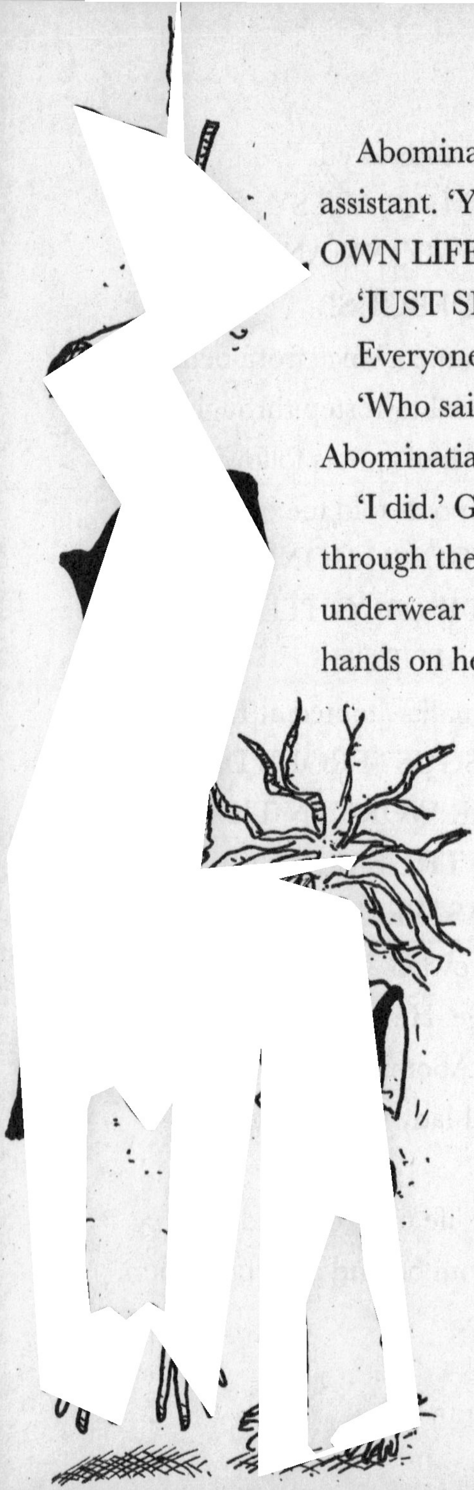

Abominatia snarled at her assistant. 'YOU MADE YOUR OWN LIFE MISEROUS, YOU –'

'JUST SHUT UP!' came a voice.

Everyone looked about.

'Who said that?' snapped Abominatia.

'I did.' Gruntilda clambered up through the trapdoor in her underwear and stood there with her hands on her scrawny hips.

'*WHAT* DID YOU SAY?' Abominatia looked stunned beyond belief.

'I said *Shut up*, Moomsie!'

Gruntilda walked over to where Abominatia was hanging and poked the end of her nose. 'I'm not a dungle, Moomsie! I know I can't sing, but d'you know what? NEITHER CAN YOU! I've heard you in the kitchen . . . YOU SOUND LIKE A STRANGLED SLURCH TOO!'

'YOU REVOLTIN', TWIGGISH –'

Abominatia kicked her legs wildly and snapped free of the rope. She clattered to the floor, but was instantly back on her feet, drooling and snarling like a monster at the circle that had gathered round.

'I'M GOIN' TO FEED EVERY LAST ONE OF YOU TO MY HAIR!' she bellowed as her flytraps gnashed viciously.

'Oh, no you won't,' Halitosis shouted.

'Oh, yes she will!' the audience yelled back.

'I don't think so.' A smile spread across Halitosis's round face. 'I THINK IT'S TIME FOR THE TREMUNDOUS HINKA-HURL!' She tapped her stick three times on the ground and the hinkapoots sprang into action.

Neville sighed . . . Grimble wasn't with the others.

'*Errghh!* What are they doin'?' Abominatia squirmed as they crawled up her legs and clambered round her dress. '*Get them off me!*'

'HINKA-HURL!' Halitosis shouted and did another strange hand gesture.

'*CHIK-CHI-CHI-CHIK-CHIK!*'

The hinkapoots quickly climbed into a tall tower formation, one on top of another, and grabbed Abominatia. Then, in one super-quick action, they spun her up and up, one hand then the next hand, faster and faster, twisting and turning, and then . . .

'NO!' Abominatia bawled. 'YOU CAN'T DO THIS . . . I'M SO TALENTY!'

The hinkapoots hurled Abominatia at the ceiling as if she was as light as a dungle's dandruff. She shot skywards and arched across the theatre, shrieking and howling until *SMAAAAASSSSHHHH!* – she rocketed straight through the roof.

'Bye-bye, Moomsie,' Gruntilda chuckled to herself.

There was a long silence. The audience sat there with wide eyes and shocked expressions.

Thicket, who had been watching from the side of the stage, shuffled towards Gruntilda and looked at her in her scrawny pantybloomers.

'I just wanted to say . . .' Thicket began, taking Gruntilda's hands.

Neville felt his heart sink. Poor Rubella.

'I just wanted to say – *PAAAAA! HA-HA-HAA!*'

Thicket pointed at Gruntilda and hopped from foot to foot. 'I CAN SEE YOUR KNICKSIES!' Then he turned to Rubella, winked and walked offstage.

Gruntilda screamed and dived back down through the trapdoor in floods of tears. 'AAAAIIIIIIIIEEEEEGGGHHHH!'

Neville looked at Rubella. She was starting to turn that same pink colour she had turned before.

'Are you all right, Belly?' asked Malaria. 'You're lookin' a bit . . . erm . . . rosy.'

'He . . . h-he . . .' stammered Rubella, '. . . winked at me.' Then she swooned in a heap on the floor. *THUUUDDD!*

'WOOOOO!'

Clod leapt to his feet and started clapping and jumping riotously. 'THAT WAS THE MOST INCREDIBUMP SHOW I'VE EVER SEEN . . . I . . . I . . . CAN'T BELIEVE IT.'

Other trolls began to join in and, before long, there was a huge standing ovation. Everyone onstage nervously hobbled forward and took a bow.

'How squibbly,' Malaria whispered to Neville. 'I feel all famously.'

But Neville didn't feel famously. He felt dreadful. Walking over to Halitosis, he put a hand on her arm and hung his head.

'Grimble didn't come back, did he?' Neville asked, his bottom lip trembling.

'No,' Halitosis said.

'I'm so sorry,' blurted Neville. 'I tried to catch him, I really did.'

Halitosis put her arm round Neville and hugged him.

'Don't worry about Grimble,' she said. 'He's greedier than a gundiskump. He'll show up when he gets hungry, I promise.' Then she pulled Neville to

the front of the stage with the rest of her Hinka-circus and took a bow.

After the clapping died down, the audience shuffled out through the rows of chairs and headed for the exits, mumbling in shock and disbelief.

All except Clod.

'I'M FLABBERGUSTISH! I'M BUNGLED IN MY BONCE, I AM! THAT WAS THE BEST ACTIN' IN THE WHOLE OF THE UNDERNEATH . . . WHOPPSY!'

He sat in the middle of a row with Pong on his knee and bounced him joyously up and down.

'CAN WE COME AGAIN TOMORROW?' Clod shouted to his family onstage.

Suddenly, Rubella jumped back on to her big sweaty feet.

'NOT ON YOUR NELLY!' she shouted.

Back at Home

Neville shot out of the toilet and rolled on to the bath mat with a bump. He lay there for a minute, panting, then hauled himself up and crept silently into the hall.

'Hello?' he whispered. 'Hello?'

With a sigh of relief, Neville realized his mum and dad were asleep in bed. The whole weekend had passed, but they probably hadn't even noticed he'd been gone at all.

He ran along the hall on tiptoes, opened his bedroom door and slipped inside.

'Well, that was different,' he mumbled to himself

as he looked about the room. It was good to see his toys and books again.

Tiptoeing across the room, he pulled off his backpack and dumped it on the bed.

'*CHIK-CHI-CHI-CHIK-CHIK-CHIK!*'

Neville froze. The backpack jiggled, then went very still.

'Please, no . . . no . . . no,' he whispered.

Creeping closer, Neville very slowly unzipped the bag and opened the top pocket.

'*CHIK-CHI-CHIK!*'

A pair of long green ears poked out, followed by a little hand and a smiling green face.

Neville looked down at Grimble . . .

'Oh, pook!' he said . . . then before he could stop himself . . . Neville grinned a big jiggish type of grin.

Well, boogle my bumly bits, that were an exciterous adventure. I was completely flabbergusted! Now you've reached the end of another whoppsy big Wrong Pong adventure, I'd say it's about time you brushed up on your Trollish. Try these words out on any passing trolls you meet . . .

Amatrolls	Amateurs
Amazerous	Amazing
Barrelina	A fat ballerina
Beauty-beamer	A beautiful princessy-type troll
Blunkin'	Bloomin'
Bungly	Really big
Chattywag	A good ole gossip
Chooney-chuff	An amazing singer
Chuffly	Proud
Congruntulations	Congratulations
Dainty-dinklet	Something very delicate
Dunkling	Darling

Expectorating	Expecting
Fibbers	Lies
Flabbergusted	Shocked
Globbergrunting	Causing a commotion
Grabbers	Hands
Grizzly-gripe	Moan
Grubberlumper	A big fat liar
Grumptious	Gorgeous
Heart-hobbling	Heart-stopping and exciting
Hinkapoot	A scrawny green circus animal
Honker	Something lovely or a loved one
Honkhumptious	Absolutely wonderful
Hoop-di-doo-cious	Famous
Humdifferous	Spectacular
Incredibump	Incredible
Jangled	Scared
Jumbly-Jennifer	A lovely lady
Noggin	Your head
Nonkumbumps	Nonsense
Overwhelped	Overwhelmed

Pan-troll-mime	Pantomime for trolls
Peepers	Eyes
Plonkless	Speechless
'Popped me conkers'	Died
Rampageous	Destructive
Razzly	Sparkly and glitzy
Rottler	A horrible little pest
Scrawnets	Huge insects with glowing, purple stripes
Skunkus	Smelly
Skwarker	A loud, screamy thing
Smoochery	Romantic
Snizzler	A sleeping person
Snizzling	What a snizzler does best
Toughly	Difficult
Whingerella	The troll Cinderella
Whoppsiest	Biggest
Winky	Short
Wonksome	Wonky and out of balance
Worry-warting	Panicking

Here's a few belly-bungling jokie-poos to keep you chuckling for yearlies to come. Hold on to your pantybloomers . . .

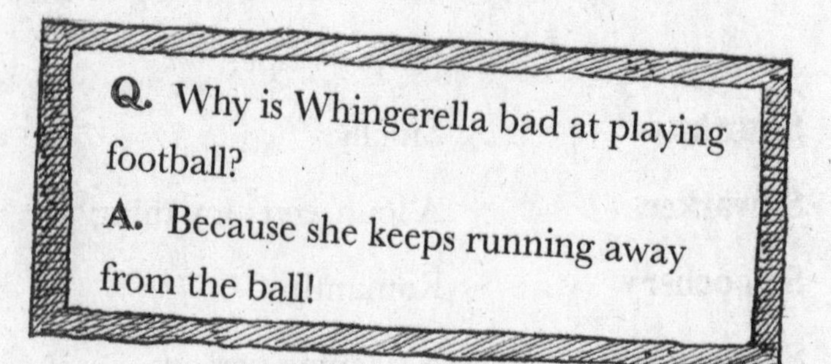

Q. Why is Whingerella bad at playing football?

A. Because she keeps running away from the ball!

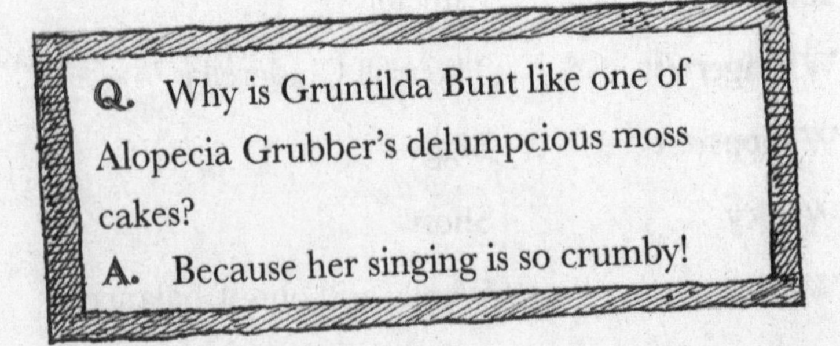

Q. Why is Gruntilda Bunt like one of Alopecia Grubber's delumpcious moss cakes?

A. Because her singing is so crumby!

Q. What do you call Rubella in her tutu?
A. Stuck!
Q. What is a scrawnet's favourite ballet?
A. Swarm lake!
Q. What did Grimble the Hinkapoot say to Neville's nose?
A. It's been nice gnawing you!

Take a peeky at these troll shows and songs and see if you can come up with any of your own.

SCABARET
MY FAT LADY
GREASEY
LITTLE SHOP OF HONKERS
WONKSIDE STORY

Pointy toes and bendsie knees
And twirly-whirly tooters, please.
You have to tap your feet in time
To make it in the pan-troll-mime.

I've seen them flock to come and dance.
I've watched them thrash and thud and prance.
But only a selecty few
Can make the grade and make it through.

And then the big rehearsals start.
I teach them how to dip and dart.
Some call it dance . . . I call it ART!
And when the whoppsy curtains part . . .

My ballerinas jump and slide
And float and soar and leap and glide.
And all the crowds, they yell and scream
Humdifferized by what they've seen!

So twinkly toes and flexy knees
And grumptious ballerinas, please.
You have to jiggle right on time
To make it in my pan-troll-mime . . .

DON'T MISS NEVILLE'S FIRST ADVENTURE UNDERNEATH . . .

AND ENJOY THE TROLLS' HILARIOUS VISIT TO THE OVERLINGS!

JOIN NEVILLE AND THE TROLLS IN A SWASHBUNGLING ADVENTURE ON THE HIGH SEAS . . .